W9-CBT-908

+
St35o

OLIVER DIBBS to the RESCUE!

Barbara Steiner

OLIVER DIBBS
to the
RESCUE!

Illustrated by
Eileen Christelow

FOUR WINDS PRESS
Macmillan Publishing Company
New York

PRAIRIE DOGS
HAVE RIGHTS
TOO!

For Meredith,
with appreciation

Macmillan Publishing Company
866 Third Avenue, New York, N.Y. 10022
Collier Macmillan Canada, Inc.

Printed in the United States of America

10 9 8 7 6 5 4 3 2 1

The text of this book is set in 12 pt. Berkeley Old Style Book.
The illustrations are rendered in pencil.

Library of Congress Cataloging-in-Publication Data
Steiner, Barbara A.
  Oliver Dibbs to the rescue!

  Summary: Beginning by painting his dog with tiger
stripes, ten-year-old Ollie embarks on a series of
sometimes disastrous moneymaking ventures to raise funds
on behalf of wildlife preservation.
  [1. Moneymaking projects—Fiction. 2. Dogs—Fiction.
3. Humorous stories] I. Christelow, Eileen, ill.
II. Title.
PZ7.S825Ol 1985   [Fic]   85-42801
ISBN 0-02-787890-2

Contents

1.

Save the Tiger

Oliver Dibbs was busy painting stripes on his dog, Dolby, so he'd look like a tiger. It was his latest project, and he was pleased with Dolby's appearance. He'd bought some of that paint they sell mainly at Halloween to spray in your hair. It was guaranteed to be nontoxic and washable.

Dolby, a Labrador and Great Dane mix, was black to start with, so Ollie had only to spray on orange and white stripes. While Dolby was a bit thinner than a tiger and not quite as graceful, Ollie thought he was beautiful.

"Hold still, Dolby. Just a few more," said Ollie, reassuring the big dog.

Bo, Ollie's little brother, held the pattern, a cardboard rectangle with a stripe cut out of the middle, while Ollie sprayed. At first the hiss of the aerosol can had made Dolby nervous, but now he was used to it. And although he felt a bit embarrassed by his new look, he was glad for the attention the boys were giving him.

When they had finished painting Dolby, Ollie said, "Bo, you watch Dolby. If you don't he will roll in the dirt before the paint dries. I'll finish this sign."

The sign, made billboard style to fit Dolby, read:

SAVE THE TIGER.
ONLY 5,000 ANIMALS LEFT.
PUT A TIGER BACK INTO THE JUNGLE.
DONATE HERE.

Ollie had wanted to write SUCCESS GUARANTEED, because reintroducing tigers into the wild had been very successful. But he couldn't remember how to spell *guaranteed,* and he didn't want to take the time to go look it up. They needed to be in the mall by noon, while it was still crowded with Saturday shoppers.

"Should we try to get Dolby to roar?" asked Bo.

"No, he'd scare people off. We'd better have a friendly tiger. We want him to look like a tiger, not act like one."

Ollie pinned a sheet of notebook paper to the back of Bo's shirt and had Bo pin one on his shirt. Both signs read, DON'T MISS YOUR CHANCE TO SAVE THE TIGER.

Leaving Bo and Dolby in the garage, Ollie slipped into the kitchen to smear peanut butter on bread for two sandwiches. He added an apple apiece to the sack. Then for good measure he grabbed two small boxes of raisins. They might be gone all afternoon if they had good luck, and he didn't want to be tempted to spend any money on snacks.

"We'll be back in a few minutes, Alice," Ollie called

to his sister. He didn't think she heard him since she was talking on the phone and playing a record very loudly. But he had covered his leaving. He could say, "I told Alice we were going," if he needed to later. His mom and dad were shopping themselves, and Alice was supposed to be watching him and Bo.

Even though Ollie was ten, going on eleven, his parents wouldn't leave him at home alone. On weekdays his mom worked until five. Alice had to come home after school every day to watch them. Neither Alice nor Ollie liked the arrangement, but Ollie figured it was better than a real sitter. As it turned out, Ollie usually watched himself and Bo, since Alice had other interests. But she was there for emergencies.

It was at least two miles to the Crossroads Mall, but Ollie and Bo had walked it many times, sometimes with Alice, who liked to shop there or just look around. The mall had big department stores and wonderful little shops that were fun for kids and grown-ups alike. The best movie theater in town was there. Today they'd eat their lunches while they walked. Even if they wanted to spend the money, Dolby couldn't go on the bus.

It was a beautiful Indian-summer day. Ollie and Bo chewed the gummy sandwiches, giving Dolby the top crusts. They bit into the crisp apples, checking out the progress of fall as they walked past Ollie's shut-down refreshment stand and up the bike trail behind their house. Lots of leaves were as orange as Dolby's stripes. All the weeds in the empty field behind their house had turned yellow. Some pink petunias in Mrs. Martin-

3

dale's backyard had escaped the early frost. Passing them, Ollie decided he would earn money mowing lawns next year. He had tried this past summer, but no one thought he was old enough to run a power mower, and old-fashioned push mowers were things of the past.

The bike trail swung to the right. Dolby wanted to stop and bark at Frank Ashburn's collie, but Ollie held tightly to his leash. "Some other time, Dolby. We have more important things to do."

This was Ollie's first time collecting in the mall for one of his causes. Usually he collected at school or from his parents and neighbors. He also donated part of the proceeds from his cider and popcorn stand to various nature groups.

He was proud of the three certificates of commendation pinned to his bulletin board. One came from Greenpeace after a successful whale-fund collection. Two were from World Wildlife.

SAVE THE TIGER money was going to World Wildlife, but Ollie hadn't been able to collect enough so far to satisfy himself. And at his age he found it hard to earn money. So he'd thought up today's project. Ollie figured adults would think he, Bo, and Dolby were cute, and donate. That was definitely the response he and Bo had received when they wore wolf masks and collected aluminum cans. The money they had gathered that time would help protest hunting the small wolf population left in Minnesota.

With the crew cut he had insisted on getting at the

barbershop and his thick, wire-rimmed glasses, Ollie knew he wasn't cute. But adults thought his business ventures were clever. He guessed they often looked at kids' ideas and not at kids. Bo, on the other hand, had curly blond hair and big brown eyes. He really was cute. All he had to do was look at people and they got out their money.

"You sure we can't have any ice cream, Ollie?" Bo asked as they passed the Häagen-Dazs in the shopping center on the corner of Iris Avenue and Twenty-eighth Street.

"You know we can't, Bo. We need all the money we can get for the tigers."

"I sure hope they appreciate it." Bo kept looking back at the ice-cream store.

"They will. Come on, take my hand." Ollie got a firm grip on Bo and Dolby as they crossed the busy intersection, first south, then east, to get to the C-Mart lot. He had decided to walk down Thirtieth Street because there was a sidewalk all the way, and it was the safest route for pedestrians. The Boulder newspaper had recently printed lots of articles about making the city safe for people on foot. Since he was often on foot, Ollie had thought of some good ideas himself. But he had been too busy with animal causes to take up people causes.

Last year he had gone on two bike rallies to call attention to the city of Boulder's need for bike trails. He knew bikers appreciated the time he'd put in because the mayor and the city council had voted for two new trails. Tigers couldn't express their appreciation for Ollie's help as bikers or pedestrians could, but on this campaign Ollie would know he was saving tiger lives.

"Let's stop and watch the prairie dogs." Bo tugged Ollie toward the prairie-dog village beside C-Mart. The Dibbses lived on the northern edge of Boulder. Now the city was catching up with them. A year ago this corner had been one big, empty field—one big prairie-dog town. Now C-Mart took up one-fourth of the lot. But the prairie dogs had moved to make room for the store and its parking lot.

"We don't have time, Bo," Ollie said. "If we don't hurry, all the shoppers will have gone home."

Dolby barked and tugged at Ollie's right arm. A prairie dog yipped so loudly he knocked himself over backward. Bo laughed. "Dolby scared him, didn't he?"

Ollie would have liked to stop to watch the funny animals too. But he had a lot of discipline. There were times when a person had more important things to do than play.

The mall was crowded as Ollie knew it would be. He'd seen that the paper was full of fall sales. For a time everything went as planned.

"Look at the tiger," children told their parents.

"Aren't they clever?" Mothers dug into their purses.

"Here, boys." Fathers dropped change from their pockets into the cans the boys held. "I'll buy a tiger."

Ollie loved the clanking sound of the coins piling

up. He figured they might get as much as twenty dollars.

By three o'clock crowds had thinned. Fathers wanted to watch the end of the football game. Mothers who weren't watching football just wanted to have a cup of tea and put their feet up. Children wanted to catch the playtime left in the day.

Ollie figured they'd done the best they could. He was ready to leave. But just as he was deciding which stairway was closer to home, Lester Philpott, his older brother, Bert, and a group of junior-high-school boys with nothing to do sauntered by.

Lester was in Ollie's fifth-grade class, and, for some reason, he took it as his mission in life to make Ollie's life miserable. Ollie didn't think he'd ever done anything to make Lester pick on him. But once Lester had gotten the idea, he held onto it like Dolby worrying a bone.

"Look at the vicious tiger," hollered Lester.

Dolby was tired by then and lay on his stomach, chin on paws. He looked more exhausted than dangerous.

"Yeah, watch out, Lester," warned Hank Huddleston, Bert's best friend.

"That poor dog," Bert said. "Cruelty to animals should not go unpunished."

Ollie smelled trouble, but he didn't know what to do. He caught Bo's hand. Then he reached for Dolby's leash, but he was too late.

7

2.

More Trouble

"Let's wash the poor doggy," Bert said.

"Good idea." Lester grabbed Dolby's leash.

The boys clicked their fingers in front of Dolby and ran with him down the mall. They headed toward the fountain that bubbled and splashed full time.

Dolby, who was a good dog and patient with Ollie and Bo, needed some exercise. After all, he had sat posing for hours, looking tigerish. He barked and leaped and scampered with his new friends.

Then, being half-Lab, he loved water. He was only too glad to get into the fountain. First he lapped up water because he'd gotten thirsty on the job. Then he barked and rolled in the cool spray. The boys flipped water at him and laughed and yelled, ignoring the sign that read, STAY OUT OF THE FOUNTAIN.

After them ran Ollie and Bo, coins clanking in their donation cans. Ollie stopped and put his and Bo's cans in their leftover lunch sack. He didn't think Lester or his brother would actually steal, but he knew that when junior-high-school boys got in a crowd, they sometimes did things they wouldn't do alone. And they didn't need the tiger money stolen on top of the trouble they already had.

"Come here, Dolby. Come here," Ollie called.

"Yeah, come here, Dolby. Your stripes are disappearing." Bo reached out to the dog, but he was too far away to touch unless Bo got in the fountain too.

Lester laughed and kept calling to Dolby, who looked back and forth from Lester to Ollie to Bo, but avoided all of them. Finally Bert and his friends got tired of the fun and ran off. Lester hurried to follow them. That left Ollie and Bo to persuade Dolby to get out of the water.

But Dolby, glad to be loose, wasn't ready for Ollie to catch him yet. Stripes sliding off his fur, his billboard wet and soggy, he crouched in the shallow water. When Ollie got near, he bounced out of the fountain. He streaked down the mall, bounding and barking, living up to his name.

When Ollie had said he'd name the new puppy Dolby, Mr. Dibbs had told him "Dolby" was the name of a sound system. Ollie had figured the yipping puppy was just that. He had cried and whined and barked for three days and nights before he'd gotten used to this new home away from his mother.

Near one end of the shopping center was a pet store, and, of course, Dolby noticed it. Kittens crowded the window, hoping for owners. They mewed and tumbled and played on a kitty Junglegym.

Dolby swerved from his headlong dash, skidded to a stop, and shook off orange and white splatters of water. Then he stood with his feet on the window ledge. He barked his loudest.

The pet-store man hurried to the doorway and shouted at Dolby. But Dolby was having too much fun to care. A crowd gathered. Ollie and Bo had to push through to get to the noisy dog.

"Dolby, hush. You bad dog." Ollie grabbed Dolby's leash and then his collar.

"Yeah, hush," Bo echoed. "Tigers don't bark."

Trying to tug Dolby away from the kitten window, Ollie turned to face dark blue pants and shiny black shoes. Slowly he looked up to see a policeman staring at him and Dolby. Ollie tried to stay calm. Quickly he thought of something to say.

"Thanks, Officer. I have him now. He won't cause any more trouble." He was so used to not tattling that he didn't even think to mention Lester and the big boys who had started all their problems.

The policeman took in the situation and then read the streaked signs on Dolby as well as those on Bo and Ollie.

"That's fine, I'm sure. But do you have a permit for soliciting on the mall?"

Soliciting? What was that? Ollie thought fast.

"We didn't do it," said Bo. "Whatever it is."

"Collecting money." The policeman explained, "You

need a permit to collect money on the mall."

Ollie hadn't thought of that. He didn't think he needed a permit to collect in his neighborhood. But now, guessing that the neighbors were tired of him, he'd branched out to the mall. Usually, he felt much older than his ten years. Now he felt little and scared. Maybe Lester hadn't set out to cause so much trouble, but Ollie figured he'd be pleased to see the spot he'd gotten Ollie and Bo and Dolby into. Ollie didn't see any way out. He'd fall back on being a little kid.

"I didn't know that," he said quietly, his eyes on his shoes.

"Are you going to arrest us?" Big tears started down Bo's cheeks. Ollie figured he was too big to cry, but he was glad Bo wasn't.

"No, but I think you'd better come with me until we get this straightened out." The officer's brown eyes were sparkling, but Ollie couldn't tell by looking at him how serious this was. Surely the policeman wasn't just teasing them.

Ollie, Bo, and Dolby climbed into the police car. Ollie held on tightly to the armrest on the door and sat as close as possible to the window. He'd never been in a police car before. He knew he couldn't escape, but this might be his last look at Boulder before he went to jail.

Dolby wasn't scared. He thought it was great. He tried to squeeze into Ollie's lap by the window. When Ollie rolled the window down a little, Dolby put his nose out to smell all the good smells as the car whizzed down Canyon Street to the police station. His head was still tiger-striped. His coat was a soggy mess. But he didn't feel like he was in trouble. Riding in a car was always a treat.

"Have some desperate criminals there?" the desk sergeant asked when they went inside.

"Better lock 'em up," an older policeman said sternly.

Dolby wagged his tail at the desk sergeant, the other policeman, and the dispatcher as they all trooped in. Ollie excused Dolby's behavior. He knew a dog wouldn't understand how much trouble they were in.

"Do I get one phone call?" Ollie had heard that on television. People who were arrested got one phone call. It was on a program he had watched one day before Alice got home from school.

Officer Byfield, who had brought them in, laughed. "Sure, Oliver. As long as it's to your parents and not your lawyer."

Ollie still wasn't sure what was going to happen. Officer Byfield hadn't thought their mall adventure cute, but he seemed friendly now. Maybe getting two desperate criminals safely to the police station had re-laxed him. And now that he had laughed at Ollie, Ollie relaxed a little too. Of course, he couldn't relax entirely. He knew his father was going to be really mad at him.

Fortunately, his mother and father were home. They were also worried.

"Ollie. Where are you? Is Bo with you? Alice had no idea where you'd gone off to. Come home this minute," Mr. Dibbs said.

Ollie wanted to go home—right away—without telling his dad where he was. But he knew he couldn't. He took a deep breath.

"I can't, Dad. Maybe you'd better come here. We're in jail."

3.

Expanding Horizons: the Alaskan Wilderness

The boys had to promise to bring in the letter and check for the SAVE THE TIGER fund so the policemen would know they didn't keep the donations for themselves. Then they could go home with their parents.

"I don't know why my hair isn't all gray by now," said Mrs. Dibbs when they got into the car. "You boys go from one sort of trouble to another."

Ollie thought they'd done a good job of staying out of trouble lately. And his mother's hair was a pretty shade of yellow. But he kept his mouth shut.

"We rode in a police car," Bo announced. "It was fun."

Dolby lay stretched across the floor in the back seat. He was too tired to look out the window and smell the good smells. He was too tired to bark at cars with dog passengers. He was even too tired to care that there was a big hump on the floor under his stomach.

Ollie thought he looked funny draped across the

narrow space. He patted the big dog with his foot, wondering what their punishment was going to be.

"You know you are not supposed to leave home without asking Alice," Mr. Dibbs said.

"I told her." Ollie knew that excuse wasn't good enough but he tried it anyway.

"Did she hear you?" Mr. Dibbs didn't wait for an answer. He knew what it would be. "You and Bo are grounded for a week."

Grounding was standard punishment in the Dibbs family. Alice was grounded about half the time, it seemed to Ollie. Of course, baby-sitting Ollie and Bo was punishment enough for her, she reminded her parents over and over. Apparently they thought differently, especially since she got paid for her work.

Grounding meant no going out of the yard except for school. No friends over. No movies. No television. No specials of any kind. Grounding was harder on Bo than it was Ollie. Bo had lots of friends in the neighborhood. Ollie didn't. Ollie's best friends were at school and lived farther away. While grounded Ollie could always read or plan his next project.

Being grounded this time wasn't bad at all when Ollie found out how famous they were at school. Bo told all his friends about being arrested. They told other kids. The word traveled from Bo's first grade up to fifth in record time.

"Were you really arrested?" Sally Carstairs asked.

"Police don't arrest little kids." Lester Philpott was jealous of Ollie's audience at recess.

Ollie's teacher, Miss Andrews, heard the whole story at second recess. She said, yes, he should have had permission to collect in the mall, but he could use the experience to tell the class what he'd learned about tigers.

Ollie gave a report that lasted a half hour. He told how there were once one hundred thousand tigers in the world, and now there were only about five thousand. He talked about how people wanted the tigers' land, and about how putting young tigers born in zoos back into the wild had worked out better than anyone thought it would.

Ollie didn't say anything at all about being arrested. Instead, he told the class about the tiger fund. The next day nearly everyone brought a quarter to school. Miss Andrews put in ten dollars. With the twenty-one he'd collected on the mall, he had $37.75. It was the most money he had ever collected.

Lester Philpott didn't appear happy that his prank on Ollie had backfired in Ollie's favor. He seemed jealous. Ollie noticed that instead of being pleased like the rest of the class, Lester looked the other way when Ollie told how successfully his collecting had turned out.

Ollie wished he could go up and thank Lester for his help. But he didn't figure Lester would appreciate being thanked. So he kept quiet.

Mr. Dibbs offered to drive Ollie and Bo back to the police station to show the letter and check for the tiger fund.

"You seem like a boy who can turn trouble into something constructive," said Officer Byfield. "I hope you'll keep doing that."

Ollie liked that idea. Especially since he seemed to get into trouble more often than he planned. Well, he never *planned* to get into trouble, and this was the worst he could remember. Usually, trouble was getting into a fight with Lester Philpott, ringing someone's doorbell at a bad time, or once when he'd spilled red paint all over his and Bo's new school shoes. Minor trouble. Police were major trouble.

"What did the policeman mean?" asked Bo in the car.

"He meant that even though you broke the law, it worked out all right," said Mr. Dibbs. "But don't count on its always working out that way. I don't want you getting the idea that crime is profitable. And ask or think before you do something crazy from now on, Ollie."

Ollie didn't think he'd decided that a life of crime was for him. Getting arrested on the mall was too scary. He knew he'd gotten off easy just having his mom and dad angry, and he felt super lucky that his popularity at school had increased because of his trouble. He promised he would ask or think the next time. But the problem with that was, adults usually said no to his good ideas if he asked first.

On Saturday the Dibbses were having a garage sale. Ollie looked over his stuff to see what he could sell.

Most of it was good and might come in handy someday. But he finally chose some puzzles he had worked, two stuffed animals he had outgrown, and a book about trucks his grandmother had sent him. He wasn't very interested in trucks and he needed money.

He and Bo bought extra cider and some herbal iced tea for the refreshment stand. Ollie got up early and baked the kind of cookies you just slice and put in the oven. He also popped corn and filled a number of baggies with it. Popcorn sold well. Especially if you had some open where people could smell it.

The day went well, but Mrs. Dibbs was unhappy about having so much stuff left. "I wanted to get the garage and the house cleaned out."

"You can take it to The Salvation Army," said Mr. Dibbs.

Ollie had a better idea. That afternoon, while business was slow, he had read an article about expanding your horizons. He could expand his business horizons. Then he'd have money when a new cause turned up.

"What if I sell what you have left at my stand?" he said. "You can give me a percentage of the sale price. That's called on consignment," he told Bo. "I sell your junk on consignment. I get paid only if it sells."

"That doesn't get it out of the garage," complained Mrs. Dibbs.

"I'll keep it under my bed," Ollie promised.

"I'm afraid to clean under your bed now." Ollie's mother looked doubtful.

"I'll clean my own room from now on. You get rid

of a job and some old stuff too." Ollie didn't like his mother to clean his room anyway, but she had made a habit of it.

He wondered if all the garage-sale leftovers would fit under his bed, but he would worry about that later. He figured each of his neighbors might have a few things to sell, but not enough for a garage sale. They could put them on consignment with him. He'd earn a lot more than with cider and cookies or popcorn.

The next afternoon he got to work making a new sign.

OLLIE'S RECYCLING STAND.
TURN YOUR OLD STUFF INTO CASH.
SELL WITH ME.

The idea started to work fairly well. But there was a lot more paperwork than Ollie liked. He had to keep track of things people brought him and how much he owed people. Donors usually priced their own stuff; then he took 10 percent for his store when he sold the merchandise. There was a lot of math, but at least it had to do with his percentage rather than some made-up problems in a book.

Alice kept coming by and saying how tacky the stand looked. "My, I surely hope none of my friends come over here and think we're so poor we have to sell rummage all the time."

She said rummage the same way you'd say garbage. Then she *hummmphed* and walked off when Ollie told her he'd made four dollars already. He wished he'd kept his mouth shut. Now she'd come around wanting to borrow money and she already owed him two-fifty. For a ninth-grader she didn't handle her finances very well, Ollie thought. How could she make all that money baby-sitting and always be broke? Maybe in a couple of years he could take up baby-sitting. It paid really well.

Running the stand didn't leave Ollie a lot of time to play or ride his bicycle. But for two weeks the weather was beautiful and business was good. Neighbors stopped and shopped. Rebecca Sawyer rode her bike over from Floral Way to see Ollie's "rummage." He'd told her how successful the business was at recess one day. She ended up buying some yarn scraps to knit a scarf for her new bear. She had this great collection of teddy bears. She made costumes for them as if they were dolls. Someday, she said, she was going to be a costume designer for movies or television.

Lester rode his bike past the stand really fast at least once a day. But to Ollie's relief, he never stopped.

People sightseeing in the neighborhood often got out of their cars to browse. One person's junk certainly seemed to be someone else's treasure.

By the second Saturday Ollie's stock was low. The business was too successful. Where could he get more junk? Maybe he should advertise. He could print some flyers while he sat there. Then he'd pay Bo and his two friends, Alvin Stenboom and Gary Gravenstein, to deliver them around the neighborhood.

He worked on what the flyer would say until finally he was pleased with it.

RECYCLE YOUR GOOD JUNK WITH OLLIE.
NOT ENOUGH FOR A GARAGE SALE?
LET OLLIE SELL IT FOR YOU.
LOW COMMISSIONS.
FRIENDLY PICKUP AND DELIVERY.

By delivery, he meant money, not people's junk, but he'd seen that in ads and thought it looked good. He put his phone number on the bottom of the ad. Then he copied it twenty times. It took longer than he'd planned, but he had few customers and it was a good way to keep busy at the stand. He wanted to avoid duplicating at one of those copy places, even if it was a business expense.

He paid Bo, Alvin, and Gary one cent apiece per flyer—adding a penny extra to make it come out three ways—to put them on the doorsteps of neighbors off Oakwood Street. People on Ollie's street knew he was there. "Remember, it's against the law to put it in a mailbox," Ollie warned the boys. He had read that in a newspaper. "We don't need any more trouble."

"We don't want to be arrested again," agreed Bo.

As they walked off he could hear Bo telling Alvin and Gary the story of riding in the police car again. Bo was making that happening last longer than Ollie had been able to. Fifth-graders aren't impressed by anything for long.

After the boys left, Ollie got bored. No customers stopped by. It was hot for October. Dolby slept, twitching as he dreamed, in the shade under the two wide boards of the recycling stand. They stretched between the two apple crates Ollie had bought at the grocery store. Ollie's father remembered when you could get orange crates free, and they were good, strong wooden boxes. Ollie figured lots of good stuff used to be free. But not much was free these days.

If he had something free for shoppers, maybe he'd get more customers. But what? If he had to buy something to give away, that would cut into his profits.

Free. Free. The word went around and around in his head. Flowers? Another frost had nipped all but the hardiest of the mums. Refreshments? The little kids would swarm around and handle everything as well as eat up all the cookies. He imagined himself on the mall and went around to every store.

Free. What was free? Discount tickets? No, free to kids too. The bubbling fountain. Colored lights. Music.

Music. That was it. He'd have free music at his stand.

Picking up his cashbox, he ran for the house, looking back as he went in the door. No customers. From upstairs he looked out his window. Still no customers. He folded up his portable record player. He'd need at least two extension cords. He looked out the downstairs window. No customers. Then he ran for the hall closet and dug until he found two extension cords.

There was an outlet outside on the patio for the hedge clippers and the ice-cream freezer or whatever anyone wanted to plug in. Flipping up the cover he plugged in one cord and stretched it as far as it would go. Then he plugged in the next cord. Fortunately, the front yard wasn't too big. Two extension cords and the record player cord allowed the player to sit on an extra lawn chair close to the corner of the stand.

Ollie looked up and down the street. No customers in sight. But there will be, he thought, as he ran back to his room and looked over his record collection. Everyone likes music.

A marching band? Possible. He took that record. A storyteller? No, you had to be close to hear the story. And you might listen to the story instead of shopping. A Halloween horror house? He laughed. No. Then he saw his favorite record. On one side Robert Redford talked about wolves and said they were in danger of extinction. On the other side wolves howled in ones, twos, and threes.

Back outside he turned the player on and the volume up as loud as it would go. He let it warm up so it wouldn't whine. Then he set the wolf record on it and placed the needle carefully on the edge.

"*A-oooooooooo. A-ooooooooo. A-oooooooooo.*" It sounded wonderful outside. Why hadn't Ollie thought to play it out of doors before?

"*A-oooooooooooo. A-ooooooooo. A-ooooooooooo.*"

Dolby didn't think it sounded wonderful at all. He never liked the record when it played inside. The combination of the hated sounds and the surprise of hearing it in his dream about chasing rabbits was too much.

He jumped up, knocking his back against the boards of the stand. Never too steady on the apple crates, the whole length of the makeshift table turned over, spilling toys, books, puzzles, worn clothing—every bit of merchandise—onto the sidewalk.

"Dolby. Now see what you've done!" Ollie ran to set the boards back up before the customers came.

"*A-oooooooooooo. A-ooooooooooo. A-ooooooooooo.*"

Behind him the record continued.

At first Dolby barked at the record. Then he did something Ollie had never seen him do before. He sat on his haunches, tipped up his nose, and howled along with the record.

Next door, the German shepherd, who had been sound asleep under a bush, joined in. "*A-ooooooooooo. A-ooooooooooo.*"

Three doors down, Shiska, part husky, part wolf herself, answered the wild call of her ancestors. "*A-ooooooooooo. A-ooooooooooo.*"

From down the street and toward the stand ran two dogs, one a chubby golden retriever who terrorized the neighborhood garbage cans, one a shelty that Ollie had never before seen loose.

The city of Boulder did have a leash law, and people paid attention to it when they walked their dogs or when they were downtown. At home, where most dogs were penned or well trained to stay inside yards, owners were less careful.

"*A-ooooooooo. A-oooooooo.*" There was a call of the wild in the howling that made every dog within blocks forget his or her training. Those who couldn't get loose joined in the barking and howling. The others left home to see where the hunting party was gathering.

By the time Ollie realized what was happening and jerked the needle off the record, it was too late. His front yard was the center of the Alaskan wilderness, every dog's fantasy of adventure and freedom.

4.

Think Before You Act

Turning off the wolf howls didn't help. Once the music was gone, the dogs started to notice each other. They sniffed warily.

Dolby realized his yard—his territory—was being invaded. He started to growl.

Oh, no, Ollie thought. All he needed was a ten-dog fight. Quickly he set the needle back on the record. It would keep the dogs entertained until he was able to catch them and deliver them back home.

"A-ooooooooo. A-ooooooooo. A-ooooooooooo." The fascinating noise started again. Some of the dogs began to howl with the record. Others just sat and listened.

"Ollie! Whatever is going on?" Alice burst out of the house. "I was in a very important conversation." Her hair was in curlers and she held out one hand, drying her fingernail polish.

"Help me catch dogs, Alice. We have to take them home or they'll fight."

"Turn off that noise."

"I can't. They like it."

Alice *harummmphed* and went to get the Johnsons' shelty, grabbing it with her unpainted fingers. She *would* take the easiest, Ollie thought.

"Hey, you can hear that all over the neighborhood." Bo and his friends ran down the sidewalk and stopped by the toppled recycling stand. "It's neat."

"Yeah, but I need help. Bo, you get Honey. Alvin and Gary, take your pick. They have to go home."

Ollie was good at organization. If he had enough help he could get the dogs returned home before his parents got back and killed him. He took hold of Dolby's collar and tugged him toward the house.

Dolby was enjoying his party. He didn't want to go inside. He sat down and dragged his bottom along the lawn.

"Come on, Dolby. This is no party." Ollie turned around and pulled with both hands as he pleaded with the big dog.

Then he bumped into a tree that hadn't been there before. He looked around. It wasn't a tree. Trees don't wear dark blue pants and shiny black shoes.

"Haven't we met before?" Officer Byfield asked. He was smiling.

Ollie was glad it was someone he knew. But why? Why did these things happen to Ollie?

"We got a call at the station about someone disturbing the peace in this neighborhood. Do you think it could be here? I followed my ears."

What could Ollie say? He could see how the wolf

concert might disturb someone who wasn't a wolf fan. Boulder wasn't the wilds of Alaska. People liked their neighborhoods pretty tame.

While Ollie wondered what to do or say, his parents' Honda pulled up in the driveway. Mr. and Mrs. Dibbs had been playing tennis. They jumped out and ran to where Ollie and Officer Byfield talked. Well, Officer Byfield talked. Ollie listened.

"Ollie! Now what have you done?" Mrs. Dibbs asked.

"I just wanted to attract customers," Ollie said.

"A-ooooooooooo. A-ooooooooooo. A-ooooooooooo." Three wolves howled in harmony.

"Turn off that record," Mr. Dibbs shouted to Alice, who had come back into the yard.

Alice did as told, and with Bo and his friends back, Mr. and Mrs. Dibbs, and five neighbors, there were enough people to take control of a dog each. In fact, now there were people left over.

"I suppose I can write this up as under control?" Officer Byfield commented. "And I doubt it will happen again?"

"No, sir." Ollie said, handing Dolby's collar to Alice.

"Something else will." Alice put in her two cents. Ollie gave her a dirty look.

Officer Byfield stopped at the tumbled recycling stand as he left the driveway and got to the sidewalk near his car.

There was a litter law in Boulder, Ollie knew from signs he saw all over town. Would the policeman think his stand was litter?

He ran out to the street. "I was just getting ready to pick all that up when the dogs came." Maybe if he explained it . . . .

"I assume this isn't a permanent business," Officer Byfield said. "You need a license for a permanent business."

Ollie knew garage sales weren't against the law. "It's a kind of garage sale," he explained some more.

"*Ummmm.*" The policeman nodded. "Tell me, Oliver. Do you have any explanation why all your ideas backfire?"

"No, sir. They seem like good ideas."

"Maybe you need to do more thinking before you act. Will you try that?"

"I sure will," Ollie agreed. He reached for a crumpled lampshade. The lampshade looked like he felt. He could never have thought ahead to what happened when he put on the record. Some things were beyond thinking up. But he'd try.

Lester Philpott stood watching from across the street. He had a big grin on his face. "What's the matter, Wolfman. Wasn't your new idea a howling success?" He collapsed with laughter.

Ollie wondered. Surely not. Surely Lester hadn't been the one who called the police. He'd never know for sure, but somehow Lester always showed up when Ollie had trouble.

Dinnertime was very quiet. Finally Ollie figured he'd get it over with.

"Am I grounded?" he asked.

Mr. Dibbs cleared his throat. "Well, Ollie. Your mother and I have talked it over. Grounding is to help you to remember not to do something again. Like going off without telling us. We don't think you'll repeat today's . . . activity. So we see no reason to ground you."

Somehow the news didn't make Ollie feel much better.

"Could you just try, though, Ollie," continued Mr. Dibbs, "try to think out what might happen as a result of your actions?"

Ollie nodded. No one understood how hard it was.

Halloween was just down the road, and Ollie had some good ideas for costumes, but all of them would cost something. He felt he'd stay in the recycling business for a few more days. So that night after supper he accepted the calls that came as a result of his advertisement. He agreed to pick up stuff to sell.

"Is this the Wolfman?" one caller asked.

Ollie didn't think that was funny. Had Lester spread that nickname?

"This is Oliver Dibbs. I'm in the recycling business. Do you have merchandise to sell on consignment?"

"Do you think you could sell puppies?" the caller continued.

Think. Think about that. Could anything happen if Ollie tried to sell puppies? "Let me think it over," Ollie finally said. "I don't usually take anything alive. I'll call you after lunch tomorrow." He took the man's number.

On one page in his record book he wrote: LIVE PUP-PIES. A list beside that he headed: WHAT COULD HAPPEN.

They could get loose.

One could get in the street and get run over.

People only sell purebred dogs.

Purebred dogs are expensive.

I'd have to pay for one if anything happened to it.

They'd be messy.

A puppy could wet on a customer.

He'd be wearing his blue business suit.

I'd have to pay to have it cleaned.

Little kids would come and want to play with them.

Someone could get bitten.

Dolby would be jealous.

After lunch on Sunday Ollie called the puppy man back. "Thank you, but I'd better not take live products to sell at my stand. Good luck with placing them. I will hang up a sign if you'll give me your address."

"Would you want a commission for sales?"

"No. This would be a customer service."

Ollie liked that idea. He could have a bulletin board. People could list things like cars or motorcycles for sale. They could say, Neighborhood Party at the Sten-booms on Saturday Night. Stuff like that. A public service. He would get his neighbors' goodwill. He fig-ured he needed some neighborhood goodwill. If his neighbors felt good, they might not call the police so quickly when things went wrong. They could solve neighborhood problems themselves.

"We need Halloween money, Ollie," Bo said. He and Alvin and Gary were hanging around the stand. Business was slow again, but Ollie had brought two books to read today.

"Find something to sell," Ollie advised. "Old toys sell easily. Find some things for me to sell and I'll include you in my best Halloween idea ever." Ollie didn't have a best Halloween idea yet, but he figured he would. Halloween was his favorite holiday of the year.

"What is it?" Bo jumped up and down. He loved Ollie's ideas and Ollie knew it.

"I'll tell you later," Ollie promised. "But I'll need money too, to make good costumes. So find things to sell."

"I've looked and looked," Bo said.

"You must all have toys you've outgrown. Puzzles, pull toys, stuffed animals. You're too big to sleep with that bear, Bo."

Bo slept with a Paddington Bear. He had, since he was a baby, but this was his second one. The first had fallen apart.

"I guess I am."

"Do you sleep with a bear, Gary?" Ollie asked.

"Of course not," Gary answered.

"He sleeps with an elephant," Alvin told.

"I do not. It just sits on my bed every night."

The three boys went off. Maybe they'd let Ollie read now. He liked them. Bo was a good brother. But sometimes he liked to be alone, and Bo hung around him so much of the time. Lately Bo, Alvin, and Gary hung around him a lot. They said he thought of good things to do, and that exciting things happened around Ollie.

That was true, but Ollie didn't plan it that way.

Ollie felt proud of the puppy decision. He'd thought before he acted on the offer. He'd turned it down. There were too many possible problems.

In a half hour the boys were back. Each carried a stuffed toy: Bo his bear; Gary, Boris the Elephant; and Alvin, a shabby camel.

"We made a plan," Bo said. "We're all too big to sleep with these toys so we're going to put them up for sale. Gary said he would if I would."

"Are you sure?" Ollie wanted them to think before they acted. He said so. "You should think before you do this."

"We thought," Bo said. "We are all nearly eight years old. Good grief, we don't need to sleep with any old stuffed toys."

"Okay. What prices do you want?"

"Face paint costs a dollar," Gary said.

"And teeth," reminded Alvin.

"Fake blood," added Bo. "Two dollars each."

"That might be too much," Ollie said. "These animals are pretty old. Pretty used up."

"I have fifty cents." Gary pulled some change from his pocket.

The boys compared their savings and decided that if they bought the paint and the blood together, they'd need less money.

"One-fifty and no less," said Bo.

"Okay, I'll try." Ollie put a price sticker on each animal and put it on the table. "Now go find something else to do. Play checkers or something."

"Checkers takes only two," Alvin reminded Ollie.

"Chinese checkers then."

They left and Ollie went back to his book on the theory of dinosaurs being warm-blooded. It was much more interesting than the price of worn-out toys.

Sales picked up just before closing time. A little girl from up the street, Becky Phillips, traded Ollie a very good winter coat and fifty cents for Gary's elephant. She had a note from her mother saying it was okay. Ollie had made that rule from the beginning. Kids having stuff to sell had to have a note. The coat would sell for about three dollars, Ollie thought. And parents bought clothes easily. It was a good deal. He told the little girl to choose one more thing, too, so he wouldn't feel he was cheating her.

Rebecca Sawyer rode up. "That camel has a lot of character, doesn't it, Ollie?"

Ollie thought the camel just looked old, but he smelled a sale. "Well, yes, now that you mention it, it does. But I thought you only collected bears." Sometimes he knew it was good business to try to talk a customer out of buying something. It made them want the item even more.

"I do. But I'm writing a play for Christmas and I think I'll need a camel." She picked up the camel and turned it over and over.

"It's your money, Rebecca." Ollie took the dollar-fifty and watched Rebecca tuck the camel under her arm and ride away. He thought Rebecca was a bit strange, even for a girl, but he guessed he liked her okay. She had good ideas.

A blue car stopped and a family piled out. They were on their way home from visiting their grandmother. She was in a nursing home, the boy explained. It wasn't bad, though. They had clowns visiting there today.

The mother spotted the good winter coat right away. Then she bought all of Alice's outgrown sweaters. Alice had been too busy to get them out on garage-sale day, but there was a new record she wanted, so she'd taken time today and found lots of good stuff to sell. She might find his stand tacky, but when she needed money it was a different matter. Ollie was pleased. This was his best sale today.

"Come on, Susan," the mother said. "We have to go."

"I haven't bought anything yet," Susan complained. She'd looked at everything and handled it too, Ollie noticed.

Their grandmother had given each child three dollars. Lucky for Ollie they'd stopped at the stand instead of C-Mart. But then they'd gotten more for their money at his stand too. So he figured they'd both had some good luck.

Finally Susan decided on Bo's bear. "Give me change," she said to Ollie, handing him two dollars.

Ollie was almost out of patience with her, but he didn't say so. He handed Susan two quarters and was glad to see them get into their car, even if they had been good customers. Having a store was almost too much work and trouble, Ollie thought. Maybe next time he thought of a way to earn money, it would only involve him and not a lot of other people.

Quickly he wrote down what he'd sold. He'd figure up what he owed people another day. He shut down the stand. He had a supply of cardboard boxes so he could close in a hurry when he wanted to. Some things he never took out of the boxes. They stacked neatly in the corner of his and Bo's room. While they didn't fit under the bed, his mom didn't mind since he'd been cleaning and had stayed out of trouble for several days.

After dinner on Sunday, Ollie settled in the family room in front of a comfortable crackling fire. The evening had turned cool. In fact, just before sunset, it had become overcast, as if the first snow might be on its way. Ollie hoped it wouldn't snow for Halloween as it did so often. Then the day after would be fine.

A nearly completed jigsaw puzzle was laid out on a card table in the family room. Mrs. Dibbs was a jigsaw-puzzle addict. While Ollie preferred watching a few television shows to playing with a puzzle, he liked them too. He and his mom had worked the red barn on this one and some of the orange trees inside the frame, but this puzzle was hard. All the autumn trees were the same colors.

"Do you have any homework, Ollie?" Mr. Dibbs asked.

"No, Miss Andrews doesn't give homework on weekends, remember?" That was one of the neat things about Ollie's fifth-grade teacher. Ollie figured she knew that kids needed time to play or do other things at home. When she did give homework it was to make something or do research projects they couldn't finish at school.

A half hour went by. Mrs. Dibbs hummed along with the radio music. Then Mr. Dibbs called out from upstairs, "Come here, Ollie. We need your help."

Ollie kept his eye on the puzzle piece he had just spotted. Then he picked it up and laid it on the mantel before he left the room.

On the upstairs landing, three boxes of his garage-sale stuff were emptied on the floor. Bo sat beside them, teary-eyed.

"Bo says he gave you Paddington to sell. Now he wants him back. Help us find him. Do you have these boxes labeled?" Mr. Dibbs picked up stuff and put it back into the cardboard boxes.

Ollie's heart sank to his toes. This wasn't his fault. It wasn't. But had he thought it through? Had he helped Bo think it through? He was older than Bo. He could think things through better. He could have helped Bo see what might happen. But he hadn't. He hadn't thought enough before he acted. His fault or not, now he knew he'd have to take the consequences.

5.

The Radio Announcement

While he was thinking through what to do, the door-bell rang.

"Ollie," Mother called. "It's for you."

Ollie didn't have to go downstairs to see who it was. But he did. It postponed talking to Dad and Bo.

At the front door stood Mrs. Stenboom and Alvin, and just walking up were Mr. Gravenstein and Gary. Both boys had coats on over their pajamas. Both parents looked disgusted at having to be out visiting instead of watching television.

"I want Cammie, Ollie," said Alvin. "I changed my mind."

"Me too," said Gary. "Boris needs me."

Ollie needed Boris. He needed Cammie. He needed time to think. He needed his head examined.

First Ollie phoned Rebecca Sawyer. He figured the camel was the easiest to get back. It wasn't that hard

except that he had to pay three dollars for it. Rebecca might be weird but she wasn't dumb. She knew she had Ollie in a tight spot—a camel shortage.

Next he explained the situation to Mrs. Phillips. She was understanding. She talked to her daughter and returned to the phone. "Becky said she traded you the coat I gave her."

"I sold the coat, Mrs. Phillips. I'll give Becky five dollars' credit at the store for the elephant."

Mrs. Phillips thought that was fair. It wasn't, though. Ollie figured it was practically robbery. All his profit was gone. The police coming was one thing. Losing all this money was another.

He was glad to see Gary and his dad on their way to get Boris, but now what to do about Bo?

The whole family had gathered by now. Alice had a big grin on her face. She was always glad to see Ollie in trouble instead of her.

"Some people came in a car. The little girl bought Paddington, Bo. I guess I'll have to buy you a new one."

Tears poured down Bo's cheeks, and he sniffed loudly. "I don't want a new one. I broke in a new one once. It was never the same. I want Paddington II."

Mr. Dibbs looked at Ollie. "Ollie—"

"I know, I know. I didn't think. But what can I do now?"

"Please think of something," Mrs. Dibbs said. "Bo will never sleep."

"Bo, that's dumb. Just go to bed. I'll work on it tomorrow."

"I want him tonight."

Ollie paced the floor. He looked out the window at the trees that now bent in a brisk wind. He looked at the fire that flickered from wind coming down the chimney. He looked at Dolby sound asleep in front of the fire. Some help you are, thought Ollie.

How would he ever find a little girl he'd never seen before? Then he had an idea. Maybe he could put a notice in the paper—in the lost-and-found column where people put cats and dogs they've lost and rings and watches and backpacks they've left someplace. But he couldn't do that tonight.

"I have one idea," Ollie finally said. The newspaper idea had led to another.

Bo looked better immediately.

"It might not get your bear back tonight, though," Ollie added quickly. "The Pet Patrol. On the radio."

Pet Patrol was a public service announcement, like Ollie's bulletin board on the stand. The local radio station announced what pets were lost. They tried to match up found animals with lost people.

"Try it," said Mr. Dibbs. "Try anything."

Ollie called the station himself. His father said it was his responsibility. And at least Ollie could take responsibility for his actions. He explained the situation to a lady who he supposed wrote it all down. Then they turned on the radio.

They had to listen to two sonatas and one horn solo along with Bo's sniffles before the announcer finally said, "We have a Pet Patrol emergency announcement."

He paused for what seemed to Ollie to be a long time. Of course, any silent time on the radio seemed long.

"But it's not a cat or a dog," the announcer continued. "It's a bear. Oliver Dibbs of 3991 Oakwood Street has lost his bear. His name is Paddington—the bear's, that is—not Oliver's. It seems he sold his bear in a garage sale to a little girl named Susan. Now he needs it back as soon as possible. Susan, are you listening? He'd be pleased if anyone who knows Susan or the whereabouts of Paddington would call him at 488-4871. Oliver can't sleep without his bear. And now Haydn's Symphony number 94, the *Surprise* Symphony."

Music flooded the family room. It was a surprise, all right, the announcement. How had the announcer decided it was Ollie's bear? He hadn't told the lady that. She decided it for herself and wrote it down that way.

Alice broke into hysterical laughter and Ollie figured if any of his friends—or enemies—had been listening, they were laughing too. Alice babbled, "He can't sleep. Oliver Dibbs can't sleep until he finds his bear. I love it. I love it!" She fell over on the couch and then rolled off onto the white shag rug, clapping her hands. Ollie thought she was being awfully theatrical. "Serves you right, Ollie," she said. "Serves you right. You really thought before you acted this time."

Mr. Dibbs put his hand over his mouth. Ollie's mom bent over her puzzle and put her head down.

"It's my bear," Bo said. "Why did he say it was yours, Ollie? It's my bear and I want it back." At least Bo was mad now and not crying. Maybe he could go to sleep.

But for a long time Ollie lay awake listening to Bo turn and toss. I'll make it up to you, Bo, he thought. We'll have a really great Halloween.

By Monday morning Ollie wished he could be sick. He wished he could stay home for any reason. But then maybe no one at school had listened to the symphony on Sunday night. They probably all had watched television. Almost everyone watched television except Ollie. His parents said too much television rots the brain. Ollie liked some of the shows on television. They rested his brain. But his family played games, worked puzzles, and read at night. Sometimes they watched a nature special. Sometimes Mr. and Mrs. Dibbs watched a movie. Mr. Dibbs looked at the Bronco football games. But they usually listened to the radio or their records. They liked good music.

Lester Philpott's parents liked good music too. They had been listening when the announcement came on. Of course, Lester hadn't gone to bed. It was only eight o'clock. By the time Ollie got to school on Monday, Lester had spread the word.

"Oliver Dibbs," Lester called out to him across the playground. "How'd you sleep last night?"

"Yeah, Ollie." Mollie Kelly laughed. "Find your bear? Poor thing. How'd you lose it? Did it fall off your bike on your way to school Friday?"

"Do you need the boards erased?" asked Ollie at first recess. Sometimes Miss Andrews let him help out.

"Not today, Ollie. I just got that stuff put on this

45

morning. Go on out and play before the bad weather sets in. You'll be inside enough this winter."

The bear story spread throughout the school. Bo probably told all the lower grades, and Lester informed the back playground. Everyone seemed to have saved up a good comment by the time Ollie got outside.

He sat on the back steps and tried to ignore all the taunts. Finally Rebecca Sawyer sat beside him. Weren't things bad enough?

"It could happen to anyone, Ollie," she said. "Why don't you just laugh about it?"

Ollie knew nothing as dumb as this would ever happen to anyone except him. And it had to be the worst thing that had ever happened, even to him. How could he laugh?

It got funnier—for everyone except Ollie—when the afternoon newspaper picked up the story. It ran on the first page. You'd think newspapers would have better news to worry about, but Monday was always a skinny paper after the big Sunday edition. Ollie figured they'd run out of news. Someone had photographed another Paddington and under the picture the headline read, "Has Anyone Seen This Bear?" It was on the lower left-hand side of the page, but still on the front. They also got the story right this time, but that didn't help much either.

Bo liked it, but the only really good thing about it was that Susan's mother saw the news item and returned the bear. She said she understood. They'd lost a rabbit once and Susan hadn't slept for a week. Ollie thanked her, returning the money, of course. He had really paid for this mistake in more ways than one.

But the story was too good to blow over quickly.

"What are you going to be for Halloween, Dibbs?" Lester asked three days later. "A zookeeper?"

"Oh, I can't bear it." Morey Livingstone slapped his leg and laughed.

"It's just unbearable." Lester kept it up.

Ollie had planned to dress as a wolf for Halloween, but that was two weeks ago. Kids in the neighborhood still called him Wolfman, and dressing like an animal at all seemed a bad idea now. What could he do? For once in his life he seemed to be out of ideas.

6.

The Halloween Caper

"What are you going to be for Halloween, Ollie?" Rebecca Sawyer asked. She had made a habit of sitting by him at recess the last few days.

"I'm fresh out of ideas," Ollie admitted. He hadn't minded Rebecca's company as much as he'd thought. It gave him someone to talk to. Frank Ashburn was out of town with his parents. Ollie usually talked to Frank if he wanted some feedback on a great idea.

"I never thought I'd hear you say that, Oliver Dibbs." Rebecca bounced the ball that went with her jacks.

"I was going to be a wolf and collect for saving wolves in Alaska, but that doesn't seem like such a good idea now."

"Yeah, I heard about that." Rebecca laughed.

"It wasn't so funny."

"It was funny, Ollie. Stop feeling sorry for yourself. Maybe you need to improve your sense of humor. And learn to laugh at yourself."

All Ollie needed was a lecture from Rebecca Sawyer. But he kept his mouth shut about her advice. He didn't want to laugh at himself. Nothing that had happened lately seemed funny to him. And there were already plenty of people laughing without his joining in.

"Are you afraid that Lester will laugh at you if you dress like a wolf for Halloween?" Rebecca insisted on asking Ollie questions.

"I'm not afraid of Lester or anyone else. But I don't like being laughed at."

"If you let the possibility of Lester or anyone else laughing keep you from doing what you want to do, that's being afraid, Ollie. And you aren't as neat a person as I thought you were."

Rebecca thought he was neat? Ollie shouldn't care what Rebecca thought any more than Lester, but he found he did. "How do you know so much about all this, Rebecca? Are you trying to get a job with 'Dear Abby'?"

"Girls are naturally more adept at social relationships. That is a known fact."

"So, what would you do?" It wouldn't hurt to listen if Rebecca had an idea.

"You could go trick-or-treating with me. We could dress funny. Like Tweedledum and Tweedledee. Or, let's see . . . Jack and Jill."

That was a terrible idea. But Ollie didn't say so right out loud. "I have to take Bo around. I already promised my mom."

"Oh. Well, let me think some more."

Before Rebecca could come up with another idea, Bo, Alvin, and Gary rounded the corner. They weren't supposed to be off their playground. Ollie had told them so a million times.

"We just came around for one minute, Ollie." Bo was bursting with smiles. "I told Alvin and Gary you were the best brother in the whole world and that you'd take them trick-or-treating too. We all want to go together. What are you going to wear? Want to hear what we're going to wear?"

"We'll talk about this later, Bo. Go back to your own playground." Ollie couldn't believe it. But he didn't have the heart to argue with Bo right after he'd said Ollie was a good brother. He watched the three leave, talking about blood and vampires.

"They're making me glad I'm an only child, Ollie. Hey, I have an idea. The wolf and the three little pigs."

"That story makes the wolf a bad guy. It helps the wolf have a bad image, and it isn't very good now. It's the same with Little Red Riding Hood and the Big Bad Wolf. The wolf is the bad guy again."

"Then how about Goldilocks and the Three Bears? You can collect for grizzlies, polar bears, whatever needs money." Rebecca was obviously thinking in terms of the three small ones, which was fine, but Ollie wondered if she'd forgotten she wanted to go with them. Maybe she didn't want to go with three first-graders.

"That's okay, but I'm sure not going to be Goldilocks. And if you still want to go and are planning to be Goldilocks, where does that leave me? Unless you want to take Bo and his friends and I'll go with Frank if he gets back." Ollie grinned. Not a bad idea either.

"No way. Let's see. I did want to be Goldilocks. How could you fit into that idea?"

"No bears are really endangered, but they've thought of putting grizzlies back into Colorado. That would take money. People have shot all of them here. I guess I could be a hunter. But I could carry a camera and sign that says, HUNT WILDLIFE WITH FILM, NOT BULLETS."

The bell rang and they agreed to give it more thought. Ollie would never have thought of going trick-or-treating with Rebecca. He guessed he didn't mind, though. If he really had to take Alvin and Gary, Rebecca could help him out.

That night when Ollie answered the phone, Mrs. Stenboom was on the line. "I want to thank you, Ollie, for inviting Alvin to go trick-or-treating with you and Bo. Mr. Stenboom just hates having to do that, and I want to stay home to give out treats. You are a dear, sweet boy."

Which was worse? Lester laughing at him, or Mrs. Stenboom calling him a dear, sweet boy? Ollie wasn't sure, but he decided Rebecca was right. He'd try to remember to do what he pleased and not worry about what anyone would think.

The boys protested having to change their costume plans until they saw the neat masks Rebecca brought over for them. She had used her bears for models, and she was a good artist. The masks were of heavy paper, and Rebecca had made ears from scrap material her mother had given her. Bo was a grizzly, Alvin a black bear, and Gary a polar bear.

"A costume designer always has scraps handy," she explained. She showed them her dress, an old recital dress with lots of ruffles that her mother had helped her sew on.

Ollie had to agree that her wig was perfect. She had sewed tons of yellow yarn on an old beanie hat and had curled it with her mother's curling iron. He still felt a little uncomfortable with the whole idea of going with Rebecca, but she had made him a neat mustache and he liked that.

"Somehow it seemed perfect, Ollie," Rebecca said of the mustache. "Gives you an intellectual look that says smart people don't destroy animals for fun."

Ollie looked in the mirror in his mother's room. With his deerstalker hat, his dad's wool checkered jacket, and the mustache, he looked good, even if he didn't fit into Goldilocks's story.

At school, the word got out that Ollie and Rebecca were going trick-or-treating together.

"Ollie loves Rebecca," taunted Lester at recess.

"Rebecca loves Ollie," shouted one of the girls from a group of gigglers.

"Good grief," said Ollie.

"Ignore them," Rebecca reminded him. "People who tease are usually jealous. Lester is jealous of you."

"Because he likes you?" Ollie asked.

"No, silly." Rebecca made a face. "Lester is just jealous of all your good ideas and the fun you have."

Ollie had trouble believing that Lester was jealous of him. But girls often knew more about that kind of thing. So he and Rebecca joined in a game of kickball and ignored what people were saying.

Halloween dawned cold but the snow still held off. For once the holiday was on a Saturday, which made it more fun. They'd had a Halloween party at school on Friday, but he and Rebecca hadn't worn their new costumes. They wanted to keep them a surprise, and besides, Goldilocks needed the three bears who were in first grade. Bo and his friends were glad to wear the vampire outfits they'd given up to be bears.

In Wednesday's paper was an ad from Albertson's grocery store, the one near C-Mart. They were giving a five-dollar prize for the best costume and lots of other prizes as well.

Ollie had suggested they try for the first prize to add to their bear-fund money. Rebecca agreed. The contest judging was at four o'clock. Ollie figured they'd get dressed early, go over to the store, then come back and wait at his house until dark. It got dark about five-thirty now that clocks had been changed back to Mountain Standard Time. Just in case, though, he told the boys to bring their trick-or-treat sacks to Albertson's.

Rebecca had taken the boys' masks home, afraid they wouldn't last until Halloween if the boys wore them. So Ollie gathered his clothes, the three little boys, and they set out for Rebecca's house. He had wanted to call Rebecca to be sure he hadn't forgotten anything, but

Alice had been on the phone for an hour, making plans with her friends to go to some horror movie.

They walked the four blocks toward school and Rebecca's neighborhood. Ollie planned to say trick-or-treat when Rebecca answered the doorbell, but Mrs. Sawyer came to the door instead.

"Oh, Ollie," Mrs. Sawyer began, and Ollie knew something was wrong. "Rebecca tried to call you and so did I. But your phone has been busy for a long time. Rebecca is sick."

Sick! Ollie felt sorry for Rebecca, missing Halloween, but he felt more sorry for himself. Their plans were ruined.

"What does she have?" he asked, trying not to show his disappointment.

"Chicken pox." Mrs. Sawyer shook her head. "I don't know why she didn't get them when the epidemic hit first grade."

"I've had them," said Ollie. "Can I talk to her?"

"Us too." Bo tugged at Ollie's sleeve. "We all had chicken pox last year. It was awful."

"And itchy," said Alvin.

"Yeah, awful itchy," echoed Gary.

The four boys followed Mrs. Sawyer to Rebecca's room. Because Rebecca was an only child, she had a big room all her own. It was decorated like a zoo. Well, more like a home for abandoned bears. Costumed bears sat on shelves, hung by swings, or slouched on chairs and the dresser.

"Oh, Ollie," Rebecca said, in the same end-of-the-world voice that Mrs. Sawyer had used at the door. "I'm sorry. Isn't this awful?" Rebecca sat in bed all bundled up in a woolly nightgown and her robe. "I begged to go anyway, but we just got back from the doctor a little while ago. He said he didn't want me to get a cold or anything else on top of chicken pox."

"You don't have spots," Bo said, peering over the foot of the bed at Rebecca.

"I had lots of spots," said Alvin.

"Me too," echoed Gary. "Even in my ears."

"The spots will come." Rebecca rubbed her cheek. "I'm getting itchy. That's why we went to the doctor. To be sure it was chicken pox. But I was exposed last week at Mary Lee Sparkman's house. Her brother has them. If it had been just a cold, Mother would have let me go trick-or-treating. But it's not."

Rebecca looked so sad that Ollie changed his mind about feeling sorrier for himself.

"What will we do?" said Ollie. "I hoped we'd win the prize at Albertson's."

"You can go without me." Rebecca showed the boys their masks. She had put them on the chair by her bed.

"A hunter and the three bears will never win a prize." Ollie and Rebecca had even worked out a short skit for the grocery-store contest. He would pretend to hunt bears. Then Rebecca as Goldilocks would step in front of them. He'd throw away his gun and get out his sign.

"I did think of one plan, Ollie." Rebecca said the words in a way that made Ollie think he wouldn't like her idea.

"Remember how we added the hunter after we thought of Goldilocks and the Three Bears?" Rebecca stopped talking but Ollie said nothing. He didn't like what he was thinking.

Rebecca went on. "Why can't you be Goldilocks, Ollie?"

Ollie started to protest. She cut him off. "There are lots of curls. We're about the same size. If you take off your glasses and put on lots of makeup, no one will know you."

"They will too!" Ollie finally got some words out. "Rebecca Sawyer, you just thought of this so that *you'd* feel better. I will not dress like a girl, not for a prize, not for anything."

Ollie just happened to look at Bo when he finished protesting. Bo's eyes were huge. He was getting ready to cry.

"Does this mean we won't go trick-or-treating?" he said.

"No, Bo. You can wear the bear masks. I'll be a hunter. An ex-hunter. No one will even know about our other plan."

"It won't be as good without Goldilocks," Alvin said.

"No, it won't be as good." Gary's face was all clouded up too.

"We won't laugh at you," Bo promised.

"Even if you look funny, we won't laugh," Alvin added.

"We promise," Gary said.

"We'll swear in blood, like on television," Bo said,

making Ollie think he saw more television than his parents knew about. Probably at Alvin's.

Bo took the fake blood the boys had bought for vampire costumes out of his pocket. He squirted a dab on top of each boy's hand. With his finger he marked an X on his forehead. "I swear in blood I'll never laugh at Ollie dressed like Goldilocks no matter how funny he looks. Ever, ever, ever."

"Me either." Alvin x-ed his forehead.

"And we won't even tell who you are either." Gary repeated the oath.

"Please, Ollie," Bo pleaded. "You can't let us down now."

Ollie was going to be stubborn no matter what the boys did or said or promised. "Everyone will know who I am. You won't have to tell."

Rebecca had kept quiet during the swearing ceremony. Now she said, "Ollie, what if you *wanted* to be funny? What if you *wanted* people to laugh at you? What if you didn't even pretend it was me? You let people find out it was you. You would *want* to be funny. When people laughed you'd know you were a good actor. A comedian."

Ollie didn't want to be a comedian. He never tried to be funny. There were people in his class who acted funny all the time. That was the way they got attention. They wanted to make people laugh. He had never, never wanted people to laugh at him. They just did. Being funny on purpose was a new idea for him. He thought it over. There was dead silence in the room.

"Please, Ollie," begged Bo. "We *will* laugh if you want us to. Try to be funny. You can do anything!"

Ollie knew that Bo thought he could do anything. Sometimes it was hard living up to Bo's expectations.

"Okay," Ollie finally decided. "I'll do it. I may not like it, but I'll do it."

"Oh, Ollie." Bo hugged him. "We love you."

"Yeah," said Alvin and Gary together. "We love you, Ollie."

"Good grief," Ollie said.

Reluctantly he put on Rebecca's yellow ruffled dress over his jeans and sweat shirt. He rolled up his jean legs so they didn't show.

Bo popped his flattened hand over his mouth. "Can we laugh, Ollie?"

"Go ahead." Ollie sighed. "Get it over with."

Amid all the giggles—not Ollie's—Ollie put on the wig. He took off his glasses, which made things better because his face in the mirror was all blurry. Then he sat still and let Rebecca put makeup on his face. She even had some false eyelashes for him. They tickled his cheeks when he blinked.

"You're beautiful, Ollie," Rebecca said.

"Okay, okay, Rebecca. Lay off." Ollie leaned close to the mirror. He thought he looked awful.

"I guess you'll have to keep on your tennis shoes." Rebecca looked at Ollie's dirty sneakers. "Your feet are bigger than mine."

"Thank goodness," Ollie said. He puckered up his pink lips for the hand mirror. He did look funny. And

he hardly recognized himself. Maybe no one else would either.

"Wait." Rebecca found some yellow corduroy in her scrap box. Quickly she cut out pieces and pinned them over the tops of Ollie's shoes. Not great, but better than the sneakers if the pieces stayed on. Ollie thought they looked like house slippers and were just as bad as the

tennis shoes. Especially with the blue and yellow
striped socks. But what did it matter?

"Good luck with winning the prize, Ollie." Rebecca
waved them out of her bedroom. "Call me when you
get home and tell me what happened."

Ollie promised he would, and Goldilocks and the
Three Bears set out for the grocery store.

7.

Goldilocks and the Three Bears

There was a huge crowd of kids at Albertson's for the contest. The prizes and free candy were a big draw. Ollie took a number and got in line. They were supposed to walk past the judges at a table that was set in front of the store.

Ollie saw some people he knew from his school and from his class, but since they hadn't expected to see him dressed like a girl, they didn't recognize him. Maybe no one would ever know who he was.

A girl from the store dressed in a clerk's uniform passed out candy after they stopped and held up their number for the judges. Ollie heard some grown-ups say, "Aren't they cute?" about the bears. Why hadn't he planned to collect money here as well as at the door when they trick-or-treated? No, it might be against the law. They probably would need a permit as they had on the mall.

Bo, Alvin, and Gary kept growling at people. Then they'd giggle and spoil the effect, but it didn't matter. If they didn't talk to people—and he had suggested on the way over that they act like bears—no one would know them either.

Finally a man shouted until people quieted down. He was ready to give door prizes. "We are giving three first prizes instead of one, since there were so many good costumes," he said in a big voice. "First prize for Best Costume goes to the alien who *made* his or her— I can't tell which—costume. Number thirty-six."

Ollie thought that was fair. There were some store-bought alien outfits. But a tall kid had lots of wires and gadgets on his head. The light in the middle of his forehead even lit up red. It was a great getup.

When number thirty-six jiggled Ollie's arm to get by and collect his five-dollar prize, Ollie turned to see Lester Philpott standing very close to him. He wore a tramp costume. Quickly Ollie looked the other way. Lester didn't even know him. Ollie smiled inside. This was pretty neat, fooling people.

"First prize for Most Creative Costume goes to the shower, number eighty-four."

Everyone laughed. A girl was dressed in a shower curtain. Over her head and attached somewhere inside the curtain was a shower head. The girl wore a shower cap and carried soap and a scrub brush. She was funny, and she didn't care if people laughed. She won five dollars too.

The judge quieted people down. "Next prize, and

the last money prize, goes to Best Group Concept. Goldilocks and the Three Bears. Number forty-eight."

"We won! Ollie, we won!" shouted Bo.

"We won, Ollie!" shouted Alvin.

"We won, Ollie!" shouted Gary.

Goldilocks pushed his way through the crowd followed by the Three Bears. But not before he heard another loud voice.

"Ollie? Oliver Dibbs? Oliver Dibbs is Goldilocks?" Lester's voice rang through the crowd. And so did his shrieks of laughter.

Ollie took the check the grocery-store man handed him. He shook the man's hand as did the bears. Then he turned around to the crowd and bowed. He put a big smile on his face as if he loved the attention they were getting, as if he loved being laughed at.

Of course, not many people in the crowd knew who Oliver Dibbs was, but they realized that Goldilocks was a boy. They clapped their hands as they had for the other winners. Then they turned their attention to the other prizes: coupons from the store for things like ice cream, deli food, pet food, and hot dogs.

Lester kept his attention on Ollie. He followed him as Ollie and the boys started home. "Hey, Goldilocks. Who does your hair? What long lashes you have."

Ollie ignored him. He kept remembering and repeating to himself Rebecca's words: "Lester is jealous of you."

Frank Ashburn had come back from vacation in time for Halloween. He caught up to Ollie and Lester. "Hey,

Ollie. I never would have thought you'd do that. Dress like a girl. You look really funny. And you won a prize. Great. Where's Rebecca?" Apparently Frank had heard that Rebecca was supposed to be Goldilocks. Maybe he had stopped at Ollie's before he came over to the store.

"She's sick." Ollie spoke for the first time. "Want to go trick-or-treating with us?"

"Sure," Frank said. "I tried to call you, but you had already gone to Rebecca's."

"We won, didn't we, Ollie?" Bo took Ollie's hand as they crossed Iris Avenue and headed for their neighborhood.

"Yeah, we did." Ollie looked around to see that Lester had stopped following them and had gone back to the store.

Ignoring him had helped. And Frank hadn't laughed at Ollie. Other people laughed, but they clapped too. And they had won a prize. Ollie had survived being funny on purpose. He wasn't sure he would ever do it again. But it didn't feel bad. In fact, it felt pretty good.

After they'd filled their sacks with candy, gum, fruit, and pennies, they all went to Ollie's house. Frank called home for permission and stayed at the Dibbses' for a taco dinner. Alvin and Gary stayed too. Ollie told the little boys he'd give them a dollar each of the prize money. He called Rebecca and told her about the evening. He offered her a dollar, but she said to keep it for the bear fund. Ollie would count to see how much they had later. Right then he was too busy feeling good.

The next week at school several kids came up to Ollie and said he was funny. It was an idea—Rebecca's idea, he admitted—that had worked. For a change. Maybe his luck was changing.

On Friday Miss Andrews took Ollie aside. "Ollie, I want to have a unit on endangered species. Everyone seemed interested in your report on tigers. Will you help me?"

"Sure, Miss Andrews. But I don't want to be the one who reports on bears. I've had enough of bears for a while."

Miss Andrews smiled. "You can choose any animal you like, Ollie."

The class divided into committees and each chose an animal to research. They collected pictures and made charts and a big world map with strings running to countries where the animals lived. At the end of each string was a picture of an animal in danger of extinction. A yellow string meant rare, a red string endangered, and a blue string extinct. Ollie was in the whale group. He knew a lot about whales.

"I'm not sure dodos are extinct," said Lester one day, looking at Ollie.

"That's enough, Lester." Miss Andrews stopped the rest of his comment before he could make it, but Ollie knew what he was going to say. "Get on with your report. You're holding up your group." Lester's group was investigating extinct or endangered birds.

"Let's do something for the school with this information, Miss Andrews," Rebecca said. "A program."

Rebecca was back in school. Her case of chicken pox was light. The doctor said she wasn't contagious even though she still had some scabs.

"Good idea." Miss Andrews stopped by Rebecca's group. "What about it, class?"

"Or a newspaper." Peter Allman liked to write.

"I think a play would be fun," Rebecca continued. "You can help write it, Peter."

Peter brightened. A play was harder to write than a newspaper.

"Each person could dress like an animal," Peter said, "and tell about being endangered or rare."

"Ollie could dress like a—"

"Do you *want* to dress like animals?" Miss Andrews cut off Lester's remark. "The older children might laugh at you, but the younger ones would get more out of it."

"The sixth-graders will probably laugh no matter what we do," Peter said. "I want to dress like a wolf. Anyone who doesn't want to wear a costume can carry a sign or help paint and build scenery."

"Let's make a papier-mâché whale—a big one." Ollie forgot he was going to keep his mouth shut for about a year. He was excited about this idea. They might even collect money for Greenpeace.

"We could do a scene where those Greenpeace guys get between a whale and a Russian whaling boat," Sally Carstairs said.

"I'll be in charge of making the whale," Ollie volunteered. He thought a giant papier-mâché whale would be neat. He'd design it so that three people could fit inside, and there would be handles inside so they could carry it. The whale would look as if it were sailing on the ocean.

"I'll help you." Rebecca jumped up, she was so excited. "This is going to be fun."

"Okay, class. Let's get your groups back together and plan your animals. We'll write the script later. Does anyone object to this being in the all-school newspaper?"

She looked right at Ollie when she said that. He shook his head no, along with everyone else. Some good publicity would be nice for a change.

After school, though, he knew there was one person he was either going to have to ignore or have it out with.

Lester Philpott rode past him on his bike as they left the schoolyard. He called to Ollie. "What's new, Blubber? What's new?" Then he slapped his leg and laughed long and loud.

Something, Ollie thought. Something would be new. He needed to think about some way to get back at Lester. Some way that wouldn't get him into trouble. On the other hand, ignoring him was probably the smartest thing to do. It had worked once: It might work again. Ignoring Lester was hard.

He'd think about it. He'd think before he acted.

8.

Bo, the Fur Seal

When Ollie got home he asked Alice if he and Bo and Dolby could walk over to C-Mart. He wanted to get a big cardboard box for part of the whale. Just as they were crossing the parking lot to the store, Dolby jerked Ollie so hard he almost fell over. Hanging tightly to Dolby's leash, Ollie ran until he could pull the dog to a stop.

"Did you see that?" Bo said. "A prairie dog was way around here. He'd better stay in his town or he'll get eaten."

Ollie knew to hold Dolby tighter when they got close to the prairie-dog village beside C-Mart, but the adventuresome stray had surprised them.

"You're right. He won't last long if he doesn't stay home. Must be a baby," Ollie said.

"Can we watch for a while?" Bo asked.

"I guess so, as long as we're home before Mom." Ollie made Dolby sit between them, and the trio watched the antics of the inhabitants of C-Mart's prairie-dog town. It had been there as long as Ollie could remember, and he always watched when he had time. Today Ollie enjoyed them. They were funny and took his mind off Lester Philpott and the recent embarrassing events of Ollie's life.

Finally, Ollie told Bo it was time to get going. A clerk at C-Mart gave them permission to look in back of the store for boxes. They were in luck. Two stove boxes and one bike box had been thrown out. They had to drag them, but Ollie decided to take them all. He could share with the class if the whale group didn't need them all or bring them back home. He could always think of ways to use big pieces of cardboard.

All that evening he thought and thought about how to build the whale. He put one design on paper, scratched it out, and then tried another. It was harder than he thought to get it like he wanted—like he pictured it in his mind—but finally he felt satisfied.

He hadn't thought of Lester once until they got close to school the following morning, he and Bo still dragging the boxes behind them. Lester yelled, "Blubber, how are you? Blubber and his brother."

"Why don't you go punch out Lester, Ollie," said Bo. "Then he'd leave you alone."

"It's not worth my time, Bo. Ignore him."

"Blubber Bear, Ollie. Blubber Bear. Get it?" Lester sang. "Goldilocks and Blubber Bear."

Ollie didn't get it, unless Lester meant brother, his brother's bear. If that was Lester's joke, then Lester had stopped saying it was Ollie's bear that got sold. That was some progress. It didn't really matter, though. While Lester spent all his time dreaming up things to call Ollie, the rest of the class had gotten busy on their animal projects and had forgotten about the radio announcement, Goldilocks, and Halloween.

In fact, in his group, Ollie had become very popular. Everyone was impressed with how he'd designed the whale. They cut out two flat cardboard whale pieces. Ollie sacrificed one of the boards from his recycling stand since he couldn't find another. They cut the board into three pieces and nailed the cardboard whales onto the end of each piece. Each board was rather like a rowboat seat. Ollie, Rebecca, and Frank Ashburn could now stand inside the whale and hold onto the three bars. Sally was in charge of guiding them where they wanted to go.

"Hey, a whale with legs," Lester said. "A whale with six legs."

True, but in the show they could sit down and slide across the stage. Lester was just jealous, Ollie reminded himself. His group had to wear bird headpieces. Lester was a Kirtland's Warbler and was supposed to whistle its song.

Next the group took brown paper and taped it around the frame so the whale's head, back, and tail were closed up.

"How will we see out?" asked Rebecca.

Ollie thought a minute. "I know. Everywhere there's a barnacle, we'll cut a hole."

"It will take a lot of papier-mâché to cover that whale," said Miss Andrews. "Maybe you can just paint the paper."

"We've come this far," said Rebecca. "Papier-mâché will look so much better."

So for three days the whale committee stayed inside for recesses, lunch breaks, and after school, slopping gooey, wet strips of newspaper and wheat paste around and around the whale. It looked like a soggy, water-logged submarine.

"It doesn't look as good as I'd hoped," admitted Frank when they decided that the whale had enough papier-mâché or that *they'd* had enough papier-mâché.

"It'll be fine when it dries," said Ollie. "Some gray paint and eyes and barnacles rimmed with yellow and . . ." He studied it doubtfully. He hoped it would look okay. But, as leader of the group and designer, he felt he had to keep believing in it.

It took a week for the whale to dry out, and more missed recesses to paint it. But it did look better. Ollie gave it a smile as the finishing touch.

"This whale is smiling because we care about en-dangered whales," he said. "We'll tell the whole school about the whales."

"Whales don't smile," said Lester when he saw it.

"I think any whale would smile if he saw the whale group's creation," said Miss Andrews, and then *she* smiled.

Ollie wasn't sure she didn't mean laugh, but he didn't care. He liked the whale. It was big. It was gray. Everyone would know it was a gray whale. Gray whales were protected, and their numbers had grown, but some people wanted to hunt them again.

He wrote that into their part of the script. The play told about all the animals and how their numbers had shrunk. It told how people could help them out. They wrote some songs to go with the stories. Using familiar music, they wrote new words. Miss Andrews called doing that a parody. Ollie's group sang to the tune of "Farmer in the Dell."

> Gray whales are coming back,
> Gray whales are coming back.
> Hi, ho, the ocean, oh,
> Gray whales are coming back.
>
> Two million whales were killed,
> In only fifty years.
> Hi, ho, the ocean, oh,
> Flooded with our tears.
>
> The right whale is gone,
> Asiatic grays too.
> Hi, ho, the ocean, oh,
> Let's save humpbacks and blue.
>
> Blue whales were great,
> Bigger than any boat.
> Hi, ho, the ocean, now
> Only hundreds afloat.

We made paint and pet food.
We hang our heads in shame.
Hi, ho, the ocean, oh,
We must accept the blame.

Let's work while there is time,
To save the species few.
Hi, ho, the ocean, fill
With bowheads and sei too.

Gray whales are coming back.
Let's work to save the others.
Hi, ho, the ocean, oh,
Protect our whale brothers.

It was a catchy song, and Ollie went around singing it at home until his mother said, "I like that song, Ollie, but I'm tired of it. Aren't you?"

"Oh, no," Ollie said. But he quit singing. Things had gone along smoothly for some time now, and he wanted to keep it that way. He figured trouble was like the weather. A few stormy days were always followed by a period of sunshine.

He was in a sunshine period.

It seemed a shame to use the whale for only one program. Miss Andrews thought so too.

"Ollie, I've found out about a Greenpeace rally in Denver on Saturday. People are gathering now to protest the annual fur-seal hunt. They want to pass a law. But I think they'd like it if a whale attended the rally. I can take your group along if your parents would let you go. I'm sorry I can't take the whole class."

Quickly Ollie said yes for the whole group. He knew they'd want to go. They all took permission slips home to get them signed.

"Can my brother Bo go along, Miss Andrews?" Ollie asked before he left school on Thursday. Ollie had promised Bo he'd play with him Saturday in exchange for Bo's entertaining Dolby while Ollie worked on the program. He could back out, but he'd rather not.

"Sally can't go, so I guess there's room. You'll have to look after him. And put him on your permission slip."

Bo was excited about going to Denver. "Oh, boy, I get to be inside the whale too."

Ollie didn't want Bo inside the whale with him, Rebecca, and Frank, so he had to think of another idea. In the garage-sale junk there had been a white hood. Ollie thought someone had worn it for Halloween to look like a cat. He went to look for it.

"But I don't want to be another animal. I want to go with you inside the whale." Bo frowned and looked like he might cry.

"Being a fur seal would be better." Ollie talked fast. Had he made a mistake deciding to take Bo? "After all, it's a fur-seal rally. Everyone will pay attention to you if you're dressed like a fur seal." Ollie knew Bo liked attention. Sure enough, that idea won him over.

"Well, okay. I guess I'll be a fur seal."

Ollie found the hood, tried it on Bo, and studied it. If he cut off the ears or pinned them down, and cov-

ered—covered, that was it. He couldn't find Alice. Getting some money from his recycling savings, he left Bo watching an after-school special Mom had said would be educational and rode to C-Mart on his bike. He was back in fifteen minutes. Pretty good timing, he thought. Alice was watching television by then, too, but she hadn't even missed him.

Ollie had bought a bag of fiberfill. Ladies used it for stuffing when they made baby toys. Bo was still wearing the hood.

"Keep it on. It'll be easier to cover," Ollie said.

He poured white glue over the hood. Then he stuck fiberfill all over the glue. It was wonderful. Bo's big brown eyes looked enormous surrounded by white fluff. Ollie thought fur seals had black eyes, but he knew they were really big. Bo was perfect for the part. Dolby barked his approval. His tail slapped against the living room couch. *Thump, thump, thump.*

"Hey, neat," said Alice, looking up when the television special was over. Bo ran to look in the mirror. He thought he looked wonderful too. He wore it outside and then all through dinner.

"It's not every night we eat with a fur seal," remarked Mrs. Dibbs.

"Our family is probably more entertaining than some," agreed Mr. Dibbs.

Ollie thought so too. He remembered the time right after he'd gotten the wolf record. He had tried to teach everyone in his family group—his pack—to howl, just like wolves do. Alice had said she bet theirs was the only family in Boulder that sat around the dinner table howling. Ollie still liked the wolf record, but he played it quietly in his room with the door closed.

Ollie told his family about the rally on Saturday. They'd already heard about the success of the gray whale and the play, and his parents agreed that Bo could go.

"All the things you are doing are interesting and a lot of fun, Ollie," said his mother, "but can't you find some causes closer to home?"

"I guess I could, Mom. But I like whales and fur seals."

"Well, keep your eyes open. I have always believed that charity starts at home, even animal needs. For instance, I'll bet Dolby would like more attention."

"I need a new sweater," said Alice.

"That's not what I meant about charity at home." Mom got up to serve more chili.

Ollie could have said he wished sisters were endangered, but he kept quiet.

Everyone found things to do after dinner. Ollie found himself humming to the music on the radio while he looked in their nature encyclopedia for an article about fur seals.

"Ollie," Mrs. Dibbs called. "Come up here." Ollie's mother had gone up to tuck Bo into bed. Ollie was allowed to stay up a half hour longer since he was older.

"Sounds like trouble to me," Alice commented, looking up from her fashion magazine. Ollie made a face at her but hurried upstairs.

Mrs. Dibbs looked slightly stormy and definitely overcast.

"Do you have any theories as to why Bo can't get this hood off?"

Ollie thought for a moment. He definitely had a theory. The glue had soaked through the cloth of the hood. Now it had dried and apparently it had stuck to Bo's hair.

Bo loved it. He was willing to wear the hood forever. "I guess I'll have to sleep in the hood. Fur seals sleep. I'll keep being a fur seal until Saturday."

"That is not a possible alternative," said Mother.

"I guess . . ." Ollie stated his theory, "I guess when the glue dried, it stuck to Bo's hair." It was an obvious conclusion, and Ollie was sure his mother had thought of it.

"I guess so." Mrs. Dibbs left the room and returned with a pair of scissors.

"You can't cut it off!" Ollie protested. If she cut the hood off it would ruin all his work and Bo's costume for the rally. He would end up under the whale, under Ollie's feet.

"Do you have a better idea?" She paused, holding the scissors in front of the white fur.

"You could cut his hair," Ollie suggested in a quiet voice.

"Yeah. I could have a crew cut like Ollie." Bo liked

that idea a lot. He raised his eyebrows up and down for Dolby's entertainment.

Mr. Dibbs came to see what was going on. He looked over the situation and left without saying a word.

Ollie and his mother went to work. Ollie pulled the hood up, trying not to pull Bo's hair, and Mrs. Dibbs snipped.

Snip, snip. It was like shearing a sheep from the inside out.

When the white furry hood came off, all in one piece to Ollie's relief, it was lined inside with brown hair. Mother looked at Bo. Tears slid down her cheeks.

"Thanks, Mom," Ollie said quickly, "for not ruining the fur-seal costume."

"Yeah, thanks." Bo grinned as he looked inside the hood at most of his curls.

"Will you tell Bo's teacher he'll be late for school tomorrow, Ollie? He'll have to go to the barbershop as soon as it opens."

"Yeah, Mom. I will," Ollie promised. Then he started getting ready for bed without anyone telling him to. It was the safest place to be.

9.

Oliver Whale

Friday at first recess, Ollie went around the building to find Bo.

"See my crew cut, Ollie?" Bo found Ollie and ran up to him.

Bo's hair didn't look too bad. It wasn't really a crew cut because Bo's hair was naturally curly. It was a short, curly hairdo. Very short, but still curly. It made Bo look older and not as cute, but since Bo didn't mind, Ollie thought it was fine.

Saturday morning the weather had turned cold but there was still off-and-on sunshine. Miss Andrews had picked Ollie and Bo up at eight o'clock. They'd put the whale in the back of the teacher's station wagon after school on Friday, and Ollie looked back to see if it was all right. The whale smiled at Ollie.

"Just checking." Ollie waved to the gray creature.

"Why are you talking to that whale?" asked Bo.

Ollie felt foolish. He hadn't realized he had spoken

out loud. "I wasn't talking to the whale. I was talking to myself."

Bo smiled at Ollie as if to say, I don't care if you're losing your mind, Ollie. I still love you. With the white fuzzy hood on he was cute again. Ollie had told him to wear his white sweat shirt and jeans. He didn't have white pants and his mother had just laughed at Ollie's suggestion that white pants would finish off the costume really well. Ollie knew she was thinking that white pants on Bo would be a disaster.

After picking up Rebecca and Frank, Miss Andrews turned her car toward Denver. It wasn't a long trip but Ollie got restless and a little carsick. He rode in the back seat with Bo. Rebecca sat in the front alongside Miss Andrews.

Ollie suggested they sing the whale song to get their—his—mind off his stomach.

Then Miss Andrews said, "How about making up a fur-seal song?" She sang a song for them called "The Little White Duck," and they soon had some new words.

There's a little fur seal sitting on the snows,
A little fur seal doing what he knows.
He looks for Mother with big dark eyes,
crawled on the ice, and said, I'm glad
I'm a little fur seal sitting on the snows.
Bark, bark, bark.

There's a mother seal swimming in the seas,
A mother seal doing what she pleases.

She looks for her baby and sniffs his smell,
Feeds him milk and then she said, I'm glad
I'm a mother seal swimming in the seas.
Bark, bark, bark.

There's a hunter cruel walking on the ice,
A hunter cruel doing what's not nice.
He looks for baby and swings his club,
Kills the baby and said, I'm glad
I'm a hunter so rich hunting on the ice.
Furs. Furs. Furs.

Now there's nobody left sitting on the snows,
Nobody left doing what he knows.
There's nothing left but the ice so cold,
The little fur seals all dead, I'm sad,
'Cause there's nobody left sitting on the snows.
Boo! Hoo! Hoo!

"That makes me really want to cry," said Rebecca.

Ollie felt the same way. "Maybe we can give the song to John Denver."

"Did you know that he'll be at the rally?" Miss Andrews asked. "He will probably have his own song, but maybe he would like another."

Everyone was quiet for a while thinking about the fur seals, but Ollie's stomach felt better by the time they found a place to park in downtown Denver. It was quite a way from the capitol since everyone else was looking for a parking spot too.

The three fifth-graders got inside the whale to carry

it while Miss Andrews held Bo's hand. Ollie enjoyed peeking out the barnacle peepholes to see people's surprised faces. They never expected to see a whale walking down a main street in Denver.

They were over an hour early arriving at the capitol steps since the rally didn't start until eleven. But Ollie didn't mind. He didn't get to Denver often and, between the big buildings and all the people gathering, he had plenty to look at.

"Stay close to the whale, Bo," Ollie warned him. There were starting to be hundreds of people there. The fur seals wouldn't be hunted until late winter but people wanted to pass a law so hunters couldn't kill them.

The people came in all shapes and sizes. All ages. Many carried signs that said, SAVE THE FUR SEALS or STOP KILLING FUR SEALS. Babies in arms carried flags with seal pictures. Two very old people carried a banner, FUR SEAL RIGHTS.

"My legs are cold," said Rebecca. She had worn a dress with thick tights, but kept dancing to stay warm. The whale bobbed up and down as if it were in a storm at sea.

They sat down for a little while. It was cozy and fun, hunkering inside the whale. They giggled at a few strange people who mixed with the protestors.

"Look at that old lady with a grocery cart," said Frank. "She has lots of neat stuff in it."

"Is that a hippy?" asked Rebecca. One man had his hair twisted into over two dozen tiny pieces like braids.

"I don't think it's popular to be a hippy anymore," said Ollie. "But his beauty shop must be on Jupiter or someplace like that." They laughed at the idea of flying to Jupiter to have your hair done.

Every few minutes Ollie peeked out to see Bo. Sometimes all he saw was white fur, but he knew Bo was there beside the whale. They had invited Bo under the whale, but he said he wasn't cold and could see better outside.

Miss Andrews talked to everyone. She was pretty and friendly. She had said she had lots of friends who would be at the rally, so Ollie figured she'd found some of them.

Sentences like "Isn't he cute?"—"Look at that little

boy"—"Can I take his picture?" floated through the whale's barnacle holes to Ollie. He knew people were talking about Bo. Another successful idea, even if it had caused problems.

"I'm glad I'm a fur seal," whispered Bo. "Everyone likes me."

When the music started, Ollie glanced at his watch. It was a quarter to eleven.

"Miss Andrews," he called out from beneath the whale. "Is it all right if we get out of here for a little while? I can't see."

"Sure, Ollie. You can just stand beside the whale."

The three lifted off the whale. Wow. Now there were thousands of people. Ollie looked toward the band-

stand that was placed in front of the capitol steps. Denver's capitol dome shone in the sun, which now poured through the clouds more and more. Soon it would be a mostly sunny day.

Ollie knew the dome was covered with gold leaf. He had studied it at school. He wondered how much money it was worth. Then he wondered something else.

He had to tug at Miss Andrews's coat to get her attention. She was surrounded by laughing friends now. Her sign leaned on her shoulder. It said, STOP KILLING DEFENSELESS SEALS.

"Miss Andrews. Miss Andrews, where is Bo?"

"He was right here beside me a minute ago." She looked around. "Oh, dear. You said you'd watch him, Ollie." Miss Andrews looked distressed. "But I should have watched him too. Or held his hand."

Ollie knew it wasn't Miss Andrews's responsibility to look after Bo. It was his, and he had promised. But he had been under the whale. And he knew how easily distracted Bo was. He had probably gone off to look at something interesting. The shopping cart lady, the hippy, or almost anything.

Miss Andrews asked her friends to help look. She said, "We'll look around, Ollie. But you stay here. He may come right back. Ask around you. Perhaps someone saw him leave."

"Maybe they have a lost and found," a young man who had been talking to Miss Andrews said. "For kids." He grinned.

"You shouldn't have brought Bo, Ollie," Rebecca said.

"He looks cute, and the hood was a good idea, but he is too little."

Maybe Rebecca was right, but Ollie didn't want to admit it. And what good did it do now? Another day was going to be ruined.

"Promise me you'll stay right here," Miss Andrews said to Ollie, Rebecca, and Frank. "Alongside the whale. We'll look for Bo, but we don't need anyone else lost."

"I'm sorry, Miss Andrews," Ollie apologized.

"It's okay. Could have happened to anyone." The pretty teacher smiled at Ollie. The young man put his arm around her as they started through the crowd. Ollie was glad she wasn't mad at him.

"These things only happen to you, Ollie," said Rebecca.

The speeches started, but Ollie didn't hear any of what was said. Sometimes the crowd shouted, "Yes, right!" Or they clapped.

John Denver really was there. Ollie had wanted to see John Denver. But now he was too worried to enjoy his song even though it was about fur seals and animal rights and getting along together on the earth. All the things Ollie believed in.

The rally was almost over and Ollie was really worried. Where was Bo? If they waited until everyone went home, would that leave Bo standing there alone so they could see him? Since he was really cute someone might kidnap him. Mr. Dibbs had warned the boys over and over, "Never speak to strangers." There were bad people in the world, Ollie knew. But would any really bad people be at a fur-seal rally?

Then Ollie heard an announcement. He heard a familiar voice but it was very loud and came out all in a rush.

"We have a lost fur seal here on the steps," the first voice said. There were small laughs all through the crowd.

Then the second voice spoke. "My name is Bo Dibbs. I live at 3991 Oakwood Street in Boulder, Colorado. I'm lost from my brother who is a whale today, but usually he is Oliver Dibbs. He made this hat for me and—"

The first voice cut in. Ollie was glad Bo didn't have time to tell the crowd the whole story of the hat and his haircut.

"Oliver Dibbs, the whale, if you are out there, you can come get your fur-seal brother here on the steps." Bigger laughs.

Then some music started up, drowning out the laughter.

"Well, Oliver Whale." Rebecca laughed. "Shall we go get your fur-seal brother?"

Good grief, Ollie thought. Why did all these things happen to him? He figured he was just your everyday ordinary boy. But he didn't have ordinary luck.

Some people collected stamps, some baseball cards or stuffed animals. He collected bad luck and funny nicknames.

He wished he was back under the whale. He wished he was anywhere but here.

10.

Prairie-Dog Rights

Ollie couldn't win. Everything he did was something adults found funny. In two weeks he had been called Wolfman, Blubber Bear, and Oliver Whale. Of course Lester wasn't an adult, and he'd called him Blubber Bear. Probably started the Wolfman nickname too. But adults were quick to join in the fun. Ollie thought that after the Halloween success, things were going to get better. It seemed not.

Ollie really cared about animals—all animals—not just those that were endangered. But lately every time he tried to do something for them, it went wrong. People all around Ollie pointed, whispered, and smiled. They knew he was the whale brother.

"Next time you decide to make a fool of yourself, Ollie," Frank said, "count me out."

Surely Frank didn't think Ollie had planned this—to lose Bo and be called Oliver Whale. He guessed he was supposed to say, "I'm going to make a fool of myself today, guys. Don't come along." Ollie lifted the whale. "Let's go."

"We told Miss Andrews we wouldn't move," Rebecca said.

"She heard the announcement," Ollie told her. "She'll go to the steps."

Ollie was glad to hide inside the whale. He guided the three toward the steps, looking out the front barnacle hole. People let them through, but laughed and commented on their whale and Bo, and said every funny remark they could think of.

Bo stood on the steps. "Did I do the right thing, Ollie? I knew you'd never hear me calling you."

"Yes, Bo," Ollie said through the barnacle hole. "You did the right thing." He reached one arm out another barnacle and took Bo's hand.

They waited until Miss Andrews found them. The rally had finished with the song the band played after Bo's announcement anyway.

Ollie saw her talking to a woman with a camera. Then she came to get them. "Ready to go home, kids?"

Ollie was more than ready. He wouldn't quit working for the endangered animals. But he thought he'd better work undercover for a while.

Undercover. He was under cover. Under whale. Hey, a new idea was starting to come to him. He wondered if Miss Andrews would give him the gray whale. If he took it to the shopping mall everyone could see it. He could hand out flyers about whales. He'd get permission, of course, to be on the mall and . . .

"Don't you want to hear how I got lost?" Bo interrupted Ollie's train of thought when they reached the car.

"I guess so," Ollie said, looking at Frank, who had two little brothers and probably understood.

"I had to go to the bathroom. I saw one of those little green potties and figured I—"

"That's all right, Bo," said Ollie. "It really doesn't matter how you got lost. I'm glad we found you."

"Me too." Bo leaned on Ollie the rest of the way home.

"How was the rally?" asked Mrs. Dibbs when Ollie and Bo came in.

"Fine," said Ollie. He had already cautioned Bo not to talk about his escapade. Bo understood the reason for that.

It clouded back up and started to rain after lunch. Ollie played two games of checkers with Bo and then reminded him that he had two friends who were probably bored today too. Ollie needed some thinking time. He also had a new library book about tigers to read.

"Want to watch the early news?" Dad said to Ollie's mother.

All the family except Alice sat in the family room in front of a crackling fire. Alice was spending the night with a girl friend.

"Then the boys and I will make pizza for supper."

Hey, neat. Ollie liked helping his dad make pizzas. He flipped to see where the end of his chapter was. He had stopped reading his book about tiger studies and traded it for one his dad had given him for Christmas last year. It was an old book about hunting tigers, man-eating tigers. Ollie had read it before, but he liked it so much he reread it sometimes. There were hardly ever any man-eating tigers today, but there used to be lots. And tigers are so smart, it took even a smart hunter a long time to catch one.

"Ollie. Bo. Come here!" Mrs. Dibbs called out, startling Ollie so much that he dropped his book. "The rally is on television."

The boys ran for the living room. Sure enough, there were the crowds, the signs, John Denver's singing. Ollie enjoyed it more this time even though they didn't play the whole song. Then just when he figured the news clip was over, Bo's face came on the screen, almost filling it up.

"It's Bo!" squealed Mrs. Dibbs.

"It's me!" hollered Bo. "I look cute."

He did too. The fur hood and white sweat shirt and his big dark eyes made him look just like a baby fur seal.

"There's Ollie too," Bo yelled again. "Well, sort of Ollie."

It was the whale. The whale walking on six legs, holding hands with a fur seal in blue jeans.

Ollie felt a lot better. Even if every person in the whole world teased him, he was on television. How many of them had been on television? And even if you couldn't see his face, the whale, his idea, his creation was there for everyone to see.

The morning paper brought even more surprises. On the front page was a photo of Bo, the fur seal. On an inside page were other pictures of the rally and, sure enough, one of the whale walking along with the fur seal. Ollie, Rebecca, and Frank's names were in the paper, and Miss Andrews was quoted as saying they'd made the whale for a class project. Mr. Dibbs went right out and bought ten copies.

At school the next morning Ollie found Miss Andrews had pinned the pictures to the bulletin board. She had underlined her three students' names with a red pen.

"I hope it was all right with your parents to have Bo's picture in the paper, and your name, Ollie," Miss Andrews said. "I told the reporter that it was."

All right? Ollie wondered why it wouldn't be all right. "It was great, Miss Andrews. My parents loved it."

"Oh, good." Miss Andrews got back to school business. "Well, now, I'm afraid we must return to other work today. We've had lots of language arts and reading with the play and the animal reports. Now we have to catch up on our math."

Ollie didn't mind. He liked math. He got his paper finished in record time and was trying to decide which library book to read when something caught his eye.

He had brought the whole page with Bo's picture on it, in case Miss Andrews hadn't seen it. Now it was folded in his notebook. On the second page, on back of Bo's picture, was an article that Ollie hadn't read yesterday.

"Shopping center designer says prairie dogs must go." Ollie read the article quickly. It seemed that a new mini-shopping center was going in around the C-Mart that was a mile from his house. The people enlarging the center were going to "dispose of" the prairie dogs. Ollie knew that dispose of meant kill. That wasn't fair. The prairie dogs had been there a long time.

Ollie knew he had to do something about this. His mom had said find a cause near home. This was surely close enough. But what could he do? A shopping center meant money. People who built stores obviously valued profits more than prairie dogs. How could Ollie persuade them that prairie dogs were just as important?

He probably would never convince them of that. But prairie dogs had rights too. Just like wolves and whales. Just like fur seals, even though prairie dogs weren't in much danger of extinction. They weren't even very rare.

Then Ollie had an idea. He knew what he had to do. He thought it out for a little while. Thought of what could go wrong. He made some notes. Then he saw that Miss Andrews wasn't busy. She had just helped Lester with a math problem and no one was waiting.

Miss Andrews read the article. She listened to Ollie's idea. Then she said it was fine with her if he tried it. But not to be disappointed if it didn't work. She told him what he already knew about business people and money.

"More stores mean progress, Ollie. The prairie dogs are in the way. Remember how we talked about the settlers wanting more and more land? Then they wanted the Indian people's land too. They thought the Indian people stood in the way of progress. The same thing is still true today. Developers want more and more land."

It wasn't the prairie dogs' fault that they were in the way. Ollie was determined he'd get in the way of progress, the progress that the business people wanted to make.

After school he hurried so fast that Bo complained.

"I have a lot to do," explained Ollie. "I have to hurry."

"I have short legs," Bo reminded Ollie. "I'm having to hurry too much."

Ollie slowed a little, but he wanted to get his bike. He needed to go to the police station before his mom got home and asked why he had to go there.

11.

In the Way of Progress

Officer Byfield was out driving around in his car, so Ollie talked to a policewoman. He explained what he had to do. She said it wasn't against the law if they were orderly and didn't cause any trouble. "Will there be an adult there?"

"My teacher," Ollie said.

The policewoman gave Ollie a statement saying that he had permission from the police department to hold his rally. Ollie felt proud of himself. He had thought before he acted.

That night he worked out all the details. He tried to think of anything that could go wrong.

"My, you're busy," said Mr. Dibbs. "What are you planning? Another whale adventure? Or a tall tiger tale?"

Ollie wasn't ready to tell his father his plan. He said it was a school project.

Dolby put his head on Ollie's knee. In his mouth was his tennis ball.

"We can't play ball inside, Dolby. And you can't help with this project." Dog and prairie dogs don't mix, Ollie knew. He patted Dolby. He felt guilty that he hadn't had much time to play with Dolby after school lately.

Miss Andrews gave Ollie some time after lunch to tell the class his plan. He was very well organized by then. He had a list of all the things people could do. He had people in his class in charge of each list.

"A man is going to kill all the prairie dogs in the town by C-Mart," Ollie started out, getting the class's attention right away. "The prairie dogs are in the way of progress."

"That's not fair," said Rebecca. Several others agreed.

"What can we do?" asked Peter. That was what Ollie hoped someone would say.

"We can have a protest, a prairie-dog rally. We'll carry signs around and tell shoppers why this isn't fair."

Everyone thought Ollie had a good plan. They were excited about helping out. Ollie wanted to hold the rally next Saturday, so they had to work fast.

He put Rebecca in charge of signs. Peter volunteered to write a letter to the newspaper for their class.

"We should also send a letter to the company that is planning the development," suggested Miss Andrews.

Sara Abbot volunteered to write that letter if Miss Andrews would help her.

"We should hand out leaflets," Ollie said. He got Frank to plan the leaflet, another volunteer to type it on the primary typewriter in the library, and two others to run it off on a mimeograph machine in the office.

"I guess I'd better get permission to do this at school," said Miss Andrews.

Ollie didn't know teachers had to get permission to do projects. He didn't want Miss Andrews to get in trouble though.

"My neighbor works for the newspaper," said Nolan Schultz. "What if I ask him to come on Saturday and write up the rally for the newspaper?"

"Great." Ollie was pleased at the way the class co-operated. He decided he'd better tell his parents about his plans before Saturday, especially if there was a chance of his being in the newspaper again.

Ollie's parents weren't as excited as Ollie. It was one thing for him to go to a rally, but another for him to be in charge of one right here in their own neighborhood.

"Ollie, are you sure this is legal?" asked his mother. "I don't want to have to come get you out of jail again."

"I asked," said Ollie, glad he'd had the sense to do that. "We have permission. As long as we don't cause trouble."

"A tall order," said Mr. Dibbs. "Trouble usually comes to you when you fight city hall."

"We aren't fighting the city, Dad. Just the builders of the C-Mart shopping center."

"That's just a saying, fighting city hall," Mr. Dibbs explained. "But why do you always get involved in this sort of thing, Ollie?"

"Because I'm a good organizer, Dad. Miss Andrews said I was. And Mom said for me to find a cause near home."

"I guess I did." Mrs. Dibbs shook her head.

"And I think prairie dogs have some rights," Ollie continued. "Especially when they lived there first. But the prairie dogs can't say anything. They can't fight. So I will. The prairie dogs need me."

Mom sighed. "It's nice to be needed." She leaned over and kissed Ollie's father as she headed for the kitchen. "I need some popcorn. Anyone else?"

"Me too, Mom." Bo jumped up and followed her. "Me too."

"I think you're pretty weird, Ollie," said Alice. "If you get your picture in the paper again over this, I think I'll leave home. Somebody is always asking me what my funny brothers are doing."

Ollie figured sisters had rights too. If his sister wanted to leave home, she had a right to. He'd have to have a real baby-sitter though, and that might be a problem. Mrs. Rumwinkle had stayed with them a couple of times when Alice was busy after school. She was very strict, and Ollie suspected that she didn't like boys. He knew she didn't like dogs. She was allergic to dogs, and Dolby had to stay locked in the garage when she was here. Maybe he'd rather Alice didn't leave home after all, even if it was her right. But he wasn't going to say so.

Miss Andrews had some news for Ollie the next day. "Mr. Hawkins says he thinks what you are doing is creative and commendable, Ollie, but you can't say it's

101

the school's idea. And I can't be with you on Saturday. They changed my bird field trip to that day."

Ollie would be glad when he was old enough to go on bird field trips. "Should I choose another day?" He reminded Miss Andrews that the policewoman said an adult should be there.

"If you wait too long it may be too late. You can run things, Ollie. I know you can. See if one of your parents will go along."

Ollie's mother said she would be there. Ollie could see she didn't want to, but he reminded her again that this was partly her idea. She agreed to walk over early, shop, and meet him out in front of C-Mart.

Getting out his bike on Saturday, he looked it over. He'd made a big sign that fit over the back tire. When he got to C-Mart he'd park the bike close to where they would parade. The sign said:

PRAIRIE DOGS HAVE RIGHTS TOO.
THEY LIVED HERE FIRST.
THEY SHOULD BE ABLE TO STAY.
"PLEASE DON'T KILL US."

At the bottom of the sign prairie dogs paraded across the paper, carrying signs that said, LOVE ME, DON'T KILL ME.

Ollie had a small sign to carry too. He had to ride slowly to manage the signs and his lunch in a backpack. He planned to stay all day. Mom said this time Bo should stay at home with Dad and Alice and Dolby.

Twice he'd had to explain to Bo why he couldn't

come. He'd left Bo and Dolby looking very sad beside their front hedge.

"I'm in charge, Bo. I can't watch you and be in charge too."

About half the class came. Several had called Ollie and said they couldn't take part in the rally if no teacher was there, even when he said his mom was going.

"I didn't tell my mom no teacher would be here," said Rebecca. She had a sign with a mother prairie dog and her baby. The mother held a sign that said, DON'T MAKE ME LEAVE MY HOME. The big sign said, HOW WOULD *YOU* LIKE TO BE RUN OUT OF *YOUR* HOME?

Ollie told part of his workers to stand in front of C-Mart. The rest would walk back and forth in front of the prairie-dog village just east of the store and the parking lot. Each worker had a stack of flyers to hand out. The flyer had prairie-dog facts and told what was going to happen to this town.

Everyone in the class had researched prairie dogs to learn about them. They could talk to anyone who stopped and wanted to know more about the town and who lived there.

Before too long Ollie realized that Lester Philpott had come to cause trouble. He knew Miss Andrews wouldn't be there, and that Ollie was in charge. Ollie looked to see his mother still talking to a neighbor over in front of the store. Maybe she wanted to pretend she wasn't at the rally.

First Lester rode his bike around and around, annoying the workers. He would pretend he was going to run over them and then veer off when he got close. His sign, a prairie dog in a gas mask, lay by the side of the parking lot.

"Lester, stop that," Rebecca shouted at Lester as he skidded gravel toward her.

"You can't make me," said Lester. "Neither can Ollie."

Ollie worried about Lester. If there was any trouble because of him, the whole group would be blamed. And Ollie would be blamed because he was in charge. "Your rally is legal if there is no trouble," the police-woman had said.

The prairie dogs sat tall on their mounds and watched Ollie and his friends. They couldn't know they were being rescued, but they were curious. Occasion-ally one would yip and fall over backward. Ollie always thought that was a funny habit.

Then as Ollie talked to a woman with white hair, he heard, "Yip, yip, yip, yip," and a boy laughing. He turned to see Lester riding between the prairie-dog holes, frightening the inhabitants.

"That's a funny way to show you're on the prairie dog's side," said the lady. She gave back the flyer and walked on into C-Mart.

"Lester is ruining our rally," Ollie complained to Rebecca. "I don't know what to do," he admitted.

"You could threaten to have him arrested," said Rebecca.

"You shouldn't threaten to do something you can't do." Ollie was realistic about threats. He couldn't threaten to beat Lester up either, because Lester was lots bigger than Ollie.

Then Ollie saw someone coming toward them. He smiled.

"Lester, stop that or I'll have you arrested," Ollie hollered at Lester.

"You and who else?" called out Lester.

Ollie shouted back. "Me and my friend."

Lester looked at Ollie. As if by magic, he rode out of the field and grabbed his sign.

"How'd you do that?" asked Rebecca. Then she looked at Ollie. "Oh," she said. "I see."

A man in blue stood next to Ollie. "Hello, Officer Byfield," Ollie said. "I'm glad to see you."

"Having any trouble?" Officer Byfield asked.

"Not now, thanks. I didn't know you'd be here."

"Actually, today is my day off. But I live over there in those apartments." He pointed across the highway. "And I needed some razor blades. So I thought I'd combine my shopping with seeing how you were doing."

"Do you always wear your uniform on your day off?" asked Ollie.

"No, but it was handy, and I thought it would make your rally look official. I could see you from the window."

"We must look like ants from there."

"Or prairie dogs. I like these little guys. Good luck."

"Thank you." Ollie shook hands with Officer Byfield.

"I guess you would know the police. Being arrested so much," said Lester. He spoke in a smart-aleck voice after the policeman was gone. But he still carried his sign. He'd left his bike near Ollie's.

Ollie smiled and walked up to a family. "Could I have a minute of your time?" he asked.

It was nearly noon and they had given out most of their flyers. Lots of people had stopped and looked at the prairie dogs. They had listened to prairie-dog facts. Some said they'd never noticed the animals before.

Ollie and his friends carried clipboards with petitions on them as well as their signs. "Please let me stay in my home," the sentence at the top of the clipboard said. Then people could sign their names if they thought the prairie dogs should stay. Ollie would take the petitions to the owners of the property where the prairie dogs lived.

When Lester got bored and went home, Ollie figured he was having a good day. The rally had been successful even though he didn't know if the prairie dogs would be able to stay. He'd handle that later.

Then he hoped he wouldn't have to change his mind about the success of his day. Coming toward him were *both* his parents and an important-looking man.

12.

The Remembering Service

"Who is in charge here?" asked the man, who said his name was Mr. Tucker.

Ollie swallowed hard, twice. "I am."

"You're just a kid," said Mr. Tucker. "Where are your parents or your teacher?"

Mr. and Mrs. Dibbs heard what the man said. But neither spoke.

Ollie looked at his parents, then he looked back at the man in the gray suit. "I'm the only one in charge," he said in a louder voice.

Mr. Tucker looked at Ollie long and hard. No one else spoke. "Well, then," he continued, "I guess I'll have to talk to you." He turned and Ollie figured he was supposed to follow him.

"Go ahead," whispered Mr. Dibbs. "I just came to help out." He took Ollie's sign. "This is your rally."

"We'll watch your bike and your workers," said Mrs. Dibbs. "Go talk to the man."

Ollie couldn't believe his dad had come to help out too. He'd thought they were *with* the important man, that maybe Mr. Tucker had called Ollie's dad and said, "Come get your kid off my property." Or something like that. But he hadn't even known who Ollie was or that he was in charge before he came out to the rally.

Ollie took a deep breath and stood up straighter. He would act in charge.

Mr. Tucker went into an office inside C-Mart. Ollie kept following him. He sat down and pointed to a chair where Ollie could sit. Ollie perched on the edge of the seat.

"Now look, kid. I don't want any trouble with kids over prairie dogs. But those animals have got to go. We're going to build more shopping center here."

The man was young, but Ollie knew he didn't like kids. It was the way he said "look, kid," like "look, pest" or "look, trouble maker."

"Build around the prairie dogs. Let them stay. They've never bothered people shopping at C-Mart."

"There'll be more shoppers. Someone will be bitten. Prairie dogs carry rabies and the black plague."

Ollie had no answer for that. The prairie dogs could have diseases, but so do squirrels and they live in the city. He didn't think black plague was a fair argument, though. Almost no one got black plague anymore.

"You can build a high fence around the prairie-dog town."

"I can see I haven't changed your mind. I'll give you two weeks to move the prairie dogs."

Move them. How was Ollie supposed to move two dozen prairie dogs? His mom would never stand for them in their yard. Mr. Hawkins would say they couldn't come to school. Where could they go? "Move them?" he said aloud.

"Yes, if you want to save them so bad, then move them to a new home." Mr. Tucker took out a pack of cigarettes, shook one out, and then lit it. He puffed out his cheeks. Smoke filled the office. Ollie knew he was dismissed. He left the man's office feeling as if he'd lost a battle. He'd only gained a little time for the prairie dogs.

"What happened, Ollie?" Rebecca asked.

Other kids gathered around. Mr. Dibbs was talking to a young man and was showing him the petition. Ollie was still amazed that his dad had come. Bo sat on the side of the parking lot with Ollie's binoculars, watching the prairie dogs.

"He said we can move them. And we have two weeks to do it."

"Move them?" Frank Ashburn said. "How can we move them?"

"And where?" Rebecca asked. "My mother would never let me have one."

"They can't live in people's yards anyway," said Peter. "They make holes in lawns. They need someplace like a field."

Mr. Dibbs came over with the young man. "Ollie,

this is Bill Freeman, He's with the Audubon Society."

Ollie shook hands with the Audubon man. Then he told Bill Freeman the problem.

"You've done a fine job here today, Ollie," Bill said. "We'd like to have you and your classmates in our Audubon Society."

Ollie didn't know kids could join the Audubon Society. He'd think about that later. "Could the Audubon Society move the prairie dogs?" Ollie asked.

"We tried that once before with a town near the Crossroads Mall. They don't move well or adapt to a new home. We saw only one of the ones we moved when we went back to the new site. It's not a solution as far as we can see."

"So they'll all die." Rebecca looked glum.

"I guess so," said Bill. "Unless they can stay here."

"I'd never watched them before," Rebecca said. "They're really funny."

"The newspaper man came while you were gone." Lester was back. "He was in a hurry. But he took *my* picture."

Ollie felt even worse. People would think Lester was in charge of the rally. Right then, however, Ollie wouldn't have minded if Lester was in charge. He was out of ideas.

"We might as well go home," Ollie told everyone.

"Are you just going to give up?" asked Rebecca.

"No," said Ollie. "But I'm out of ideas right now. Do you have any?"

"I guess not." Rebecca got her bike and rode alongside Ollie. But she didn't say any more.

The next day Ollie looked at the pictures in the newspaper. The story said a group of students carried the signs. No one's name was in the article. But there was a picture of Lester and his gas mask sign. Ollie had to admit that it was a good sign. There was Rebecca and the field of prairie dogs behind her. There was a picture of Bo watching the prairie-dog town with binoculars.

Ollie thought and thought. He played with Dolby and his Frisbee a little. But he couldn't stop thinking about the prairie dogs. He had this picture in his mind of men putting gas into the holes and prairie dogs coughing and coming out gasping and falling over on the ground all over their town.

"You tried," his mother said at dinner.

"Thanks for coming over." Ollie had forgotten to say that to his parents.

"You tried," Miss Andrews said again in school on Monday.

Ollie didn't think he had tried hard enough. He didn't feel good about his try.

At dinner he thought of what Rebecca had said about finding out that not many people were aware there was a prairie-dog village near C-Mart. Even she hadn't known they were there. He remembered the picture of Bo watching with the binoculars.

"Mom, when Grandma died, what did you call that program we went to. You know, where everyone told why they had loved her?"

"You mean the memorial service?"

"Yeah, that's it. I'm going to have a memorial service for the prairie dogs."

"But they aren't dead yet," Alice reminded him.

"They will be. I can't think of any way to save them."

It was quiet during the rest of dinner. No one else could think of any way to save the animals either.

During recesses Ollie told his prairie-dog workers about his plan.

"That's dumb." said Lester. "You can't have a funeral for someone who isn't dead."

"It's not a funeral," explained Ollie. "People don't know much about prairie dogs. We'll tell them. It's a remembering service. We'll remember how much fun it was to have prairie dogs there where we could watch them."

By Saturday they were ready. Stores opened at nine. Ollie and his friends were set up by then. Miss Andrews came, but she didn't pretend to be in charge. She let Ollie run things.

On the parking lot, all around the prairie-dog town, they had pictures of prairie dogs. Rebecca and Peter had made a filmstrip. They took a box and put two sticks on each side through the top. They painted pictures of a prairie dog's life and pasted them together to make a long strip. The viewer could wind the film story off the first stick onto the second to see it. Peter's tape recorder told the story of the prairie dog's life. Peter had good sound effects like *yip, yip,* and the whir of an owl's wings. Also the cry of a hawk. At the end was some music and then a speech about the prairie dogs having to get out of the way of progress.

Other students borrowed binoculars from their parents so that all around the prairie-dog town they could set up viewing stands. People could watch the prairie dogs. A student was at each stand to answer questions and point out prairie-dog habits.

Signs were all over saying: THESE PRAIRIE DOGS MUST DIE TO MAKE ROOM FOR STORES. WE WILL BE SAD TO SEE THEM GO.

Ollie's job was like a secretary's. He had read a book called *The Ten Best Things About Barney*. It was about a boy remembering his cat that had died. On the school easel that Miss Andrews had let them borrow, Ollie had pinned a big sheet of paper.

At the top the paper said: GOOD THINGS ABOUT PRAIRIE DOGS. Ollie didn't want to limit the good things to ten. There might be more—seventeen or even twenty-five.

Anyone who watched the prairie dogs could think up things for Ollie to write on the good things list.

"They're really cute," said a little boy and his mother.

Ollie wrote that on the top of the list with his magic marker.

"They're funny," said a girl. "They fall over backward when they yip." Ollie told her that was because they sometimes got so excited and yipped so big.

Lots of people stopped. The bigger the crowd got, the more people stopped to see what was happening. Ollie's list grew.

PRAIRIE DOGS ARE CUTE.

THEY'RE FUNNY. A BIG YIP MAKES THEM FALL OVER BACKWARD.

PRAIRIE DOGS ARE FRIENDLY TO EACH OTHER.

THEY HELP EACH OTHER.

SOMETIMES THEY KISS.

THEY ARE GOOD MOTHERS.

THEY LIVE IN FAMILIES.

ONE CHIEF PRAIRIE DOG LOOKS AFTER ALL THE PRAIRIE DOGS.

HE WILL CHASE OFF STRANGERS FROM OTHER TOWNS.

PRAIRIE DOGS AIR OUT THE SOIL.

THEY STIR UP THE SOIL.

RAINWATER GOES IN THE HOLES, KEEPING THE GROUND MOIST.

THEY HAVE A SPECIAL BARKING LANGUAGE.

PRAIRIE DOGS LIVE PLACES OTHER ANIMALS CAN'T LIVE.

OTHER ANIMALS USE THEIR BURROWS.

Ollie began to feel better. This idea had worked. Even if the prairie dogs had to die, they would have taught lots of people about prairie dogs. People would remember them. People would remember this town. They would stop and look at other prairie dogs and remember again and again.

115

13.

The Prairie-Dog Boy

Ollie wasn't surprised to see an article in Sunday's paper about the prairie-dog remembering service. A reporter had talked to him this time, and Ollie had explained to him what was happening.

There were pictures of the service. The list of good things about prairie dogs was printed. The reporter had talked to people who said they thought it was a shame the prairie dogs had to die. He had talked to the Audubon Society people, who said they didn't think the prairie dogs could be moved. They'd tried it once before and it had been unsuccessful then.

What surprised Ollie most was what Mr. Tucker, the man who owned the land and was developing it into more shopping center, said. He told the reporter he had planned to build a play yard for children where the prairie dogs lived. The kids could play while their parents shopped. Mr. Tucker hadn't told Ollie that. He'd just said they needed the space for stores. Ollie figured he'd thought that up real quick so people wouldn't be mad about his killing the prairie dogs.

"Are you going back today, Ollie?" asked Mrs. Dibbs.

"Yes. We want as many people to know about the prairie dogs as possible. We want them remembered."

Alice was reading the article in the paper. She looked up. "Can I help today, Ollie?"

Ollie was surprised, but quickly said, "Sure." Bo had helped the day before after he finished watching the prairie dogs. He had worn his fur-seal hood and carried a sign that he had made all by himself. It read: FUR SEALS LOVE PRAIRIE DOGS. Ollie had seen him talking to lots of people. Bo was anything but shy.

"How can we stay home?" asked Mr. Dibbs, looking at his wife. "Count us in," he told Ollie.

At first just shoppers came by as they had on Saturday. Then people who had read the paper started to come. Children carried signs that read: WE DON'T WANT A PLAYGROUND. DON'T BUILD US A PLAYGROUND OVER THE PRAIRIE DOGS' PLAYGROUND.

Students from the college came. They had signs and more petitions for people to sign.

Soon there was as big a crowd as at the fur-seal rally on the capitol steps. All they needed was John Denver to sing a prairie-dog song.

Lots of people said, "Hi, Ollie. We're with you. You've done a good job."

Ollie saw Mr. Tucker come out. He looked at the crowds. Then he disappeared.

Miss Andrews stopped by with her boyfriend. "Ollie,

I'm so proud of you. Even if you can't save the prairie dogs, you have made people aware of them. You've taught lots of people many good things about prairie dogs."

"I've had lots of help," said Ollie.

"But it was your idea. You have good ideas."

They don't always go right, thought Ollie. He was so pleased to have an idea turn out okay. He hadn't been arrested or embarrassed. No one had called him the prairie-dog boy.

About two o'clock, when the crowd was biggest, Mr. Tucker came over to Ollie. Ollie was still writing his list of good things about prairie dogs. Two other men were with Mr. Tucker.

Ollie recognized the third man as the reporter who had talked to him the day before. The reporter waved his pencil at Ollie and smiled.

"Oliver," Mr. Tucker began. "This is my landscape artist, Mr. Blivens. He is in charge of trees and grass, flowers and—"

"Prairie-dog playgrounds," said Mr. Blivens.

"Prairie-dog playgrounds?" Ollie questioned.

"Oliver has given me a very good idea," Mr. Tucker told the reporter and those in the crowd who were close enough to hear. "It's a way to save the prairie dogs. We're going to build a prairie-dog playground instead of a playground for the children."

"But the children can watch the prairie dogs," Mr. Blivens added.

Ollie hadn't given Mr. Tucker any such idea. All Mr.

Tucker had ever said to Ollie was that the prairie dogs must die or be moved. But if Mr. Tucker wanted to say Ollie had given him this new idea or even if he wanted to say it was *his*—*Mr. Tucker's*—idea, Ollie didn't care. He'd heard Mr. Tucker say "Save the Prairie Dogs."

"The building for the new shops was supposed to start next week," said Mr. Blivens. "But we'll keep the prairie dogs safe. We'll start the playground for them next week too."

"It should be ready by Christmas."

Mr. Tucker stepped over to put his arm around Ollie. The reporter took a picture. "I want to thank Oliver Dibbs for calling this problem to my attention."

Ollie knew Mr. Tucker had said that for the reporter to put in the newspaper. A week ago he had not thanked Ollie for calling the prairie dogs to his or anyone's attention. It didn't matter. Nothing mattered except saving the prairie dogs.

Word spread of the prairie-dog playground. The crowd started to clap and cheer.

"Hurrah for prairie dogs."

"Hurrah for Ollie. He saved the prairie dogs."

Now Ollie felt embarrassed. But he shook hands with Mr. Tucker again and Mr. Blivens. He shook hands with the reporter.

"Oh, Ollie. I think you're wonderful," said Rebecca. She looked as if she might hug Ollie. Ollie stuck out his hand to shake Rebecca's. After all, she had helped him a lot. Lester stood close by. Ollie walked over and put out his hand. "Thanks, Lester." Lester didn't look as if he wanted to shake hands. But lots of people were watching. So he did.

"I would like to thank all my workers," Ollie said. "I am so proud of you." He remembered how good Miss Andrews's words had made him feel, so he said them to Rebecca and Frank and Peter, Bo, and even Lester. Anyone who could hear him.

Everyone forgot about the prairie dogs except Ollie. They thought about Thanksgiving. They started thinking about Christmas. Ollie didn't want to think about Christmas because he'd spent almost all his money on paint and pens and pads for the prairie-dog cause.

At school the students made Christmas decorations and got ready for an all-school program about reindeer and fir trees and elves. Ollie spent as much time as he could spare watching the workers at the C-Mart shopping center. Sometimes he watched the prairie dogs watching the workers all around their town.

"It's all right," Ollie told them. "They won't hurt you."

A few days before Christmas Mr. Blivens called Ollie. He wanted Ollie to cut a ribbon around the new prairie-dog village.

"Of course, you can," said Ollie's mother when Ollie told his parents what Mr. Blivens wanted.

"It will be your best Christmas present," said Mrs. Dibbs, "with a ribbon around it."

The day was cold but clear. Ollie wore the new sweater his mother had bought him and let him open early. It had deer on the front and back. Ollie figured she couldn't find a sweater with prairie dogs on it.

A small crowd had gathered. When Ollie walked up to the place where the ribbon was tied together, a little boy said, "There he is. There goes the Prairie-Dog Boy."

Ollie didn't mind being called the Prairie-Dog Boy now. The little boy wasn't teasing him.

Mr. Tucker made a speech. Mr. Blivens made a speech. Ollie hoped he wasn't expected to give a speech. He wasn't. All he had to do was cut the red and green ribbons stretched all the way around the new playground.

He held the big pair of scissors and went *snip, snip*. The ribbons fell away. The people cheered.

Ollie looked at the playground. It was better than he could have imagined. There was a wall, several feet high, all around the village. Every few yards there was a spotting scope set into the concrete. People could watch the prairie dogs through the spyglasses.

Inside the playground one braver-than-usual prairie dog came close to the wall and saw all the people watching. Then he gave a big yip and fell over backward. Maybe the people surprised him. Maybe he was surprised at all the attention the town was getting.

Ollie laughed. The prairie dogs might be surprised at their new town, but no more surprised than Ollie at the success of one of his causes. It would make him work harder on other causes. Maybe if he—

His mother interrupted his plans for another project. "Merry Christmas, Prairie-Dog Boy."

Ollie grinned and looked back at the village. "Merry

Christmas, prairie dogs. Do you think prairie dogs have a prairie-dog Santa?"

"Today you're the prairie dogs' Santa," Mr. Dibbs said.

Ollie guessed he was. The idea made him laugh. This had to be about his best Christmas ever. He'd been given a prairie-dog village. He felt so good he wanted to holler, "Yip, yip, yippee," and fall over backward.

But he didn't. People would think he was foolish. He figured the day was sunny. His life was sunny. He'd try hard to keep it that way for a while.